WISH YOU WERE HERE

WISH YOU
WERE HERE

Lesley Grant-Adamson

cap. 2

St. Martin's Press ⧓ New York

Library of Congress Cataloging-in-Publication Data

Grant-Adamson, Lesley.
Wish you were here / Lesley Grant-Adamson.
p.   cm.
ISBN 0-312-14075-4
1. Man-woman relationships—Scotland—Fiction.   2. Women—
Scotland—Crimes against—Fiction.   I. Title.
PR6057.R324W57   1996
823'.914—dc20   95–42577   CIP

First published in Great Britain by Hodder & Stoughton

First U.S. Edition: April 1996
10 9 8 7 6 5 4 3 2 1

For Andrew

WISH YOU WERE HERE

1

The trap had snapped shut on her several hours ago. She did not know exactly how long as her watch was upstairs on the shelf beside the bed. She was measuring time by the length of the shadows of the rocks, the angle of the sun on the house, and by the inching tide. It was four, perhaps five, hours since the door slammed.

Kneeling at the window, she watched for him. If she craned her neck to the left she could see the hump of hill near the harbour on the main island. His boat would come that way.

A sheep had died on the beach and herring gulls were busy at it. Until today she had not noticed it. There had been the house to explore, hill tracks to climb and food to heat. She had leaped with him across a rushing stream, chased over the rocky acres and celebrated with smokey whisky in a smokey room.

The carcase lay between the window and the highwater mark, a grey lump no longer sheep shape. Only the attention of the birds proved it was carrion and not stone smoother and paler than the rest. Birds spiralled down to it, squabbled, and skimmed away to scream on the rocks; or else they lifted up over the house where she could not see. For hours she had watched them exultant and fractious.

When his boat came it would come that way, from the harbour. She strained to see. There were no boats. Once upon a time the harbour had been active with a fishing flcct and business between the islands, but that was before the long years of decline. Now it offered little but solitude. This was an end of the world sort of place.

She gripped the lower edge of the window frame and pulled herself forward, squeezing her shoulders between the slanting walls of the recess. The manoeuvre gained her another fraction of the coast

1

across the sound but it hurt the shoulder that had troubled her since the car crash. She let go of the frame and flopped back.

Standing, she brushed the knees of her trousers. There was no glass in the window, nothing to bar whatever sand or dust the wind might carry. This day was still, the sea a gunmetal sheen and the sky flecked with cloud. *'Lucky,'* she thought, seeking small consolations. *'Another day I could have caught my death of cold.'*

A suspicion tugged at her mind but just then the ululation of the birds drew her to the window. A sea eagle was scaring the gulls away from their prize. They reeled across her rectangular view, their wailing filling her skull.

'Stop it!' she screamed in anger and revulsion. 'Stop it.'

Wings slashed the scenery into flashing segments. The far coastline became jumbled colours, nothing distinct, yet through the havoc she spotted the boat. A small boat. His boat. Suddenly her throat ached with misery. A tear squeezed through her lashes. She smeared it across her cheek. Smiling, she realised how afraid she had been.

It had been there all along, the unthought fear that something might delay him and he would not return that day. Of course, that was not what his note said. That promised he would be back by lunchtime. Well, he was late, but she was determined not to be angry, not angry at the delay and not angry when he mocked her, as he was sure to do, for letting the cellar door swing shut.

She looked across the bare room to the door, a solid wooden door, a door she could never break through, a door without a catch on the inside. 'Be careful,' he had said. But she had not been careful enough.

Well, what did it matter? He would arrive within minutes. All right, half an hour. The boat would slide up alongside the collapsing jetty and then it would be no time before he was trotting up the beach towards the house. She was going to yell and he was going to set her free.

The gulls abandoned their protest and flounced away to the rocks. The far coastline was clear again. There was no boat. The woman felt her scalp tighten and tears pricking behind her eyelids. She clenched her teeth. It had been a trick of the light then, a hope made into a kind of reality, a deception. There was no boat.

Far out the water became ruffled. Cloudlets merged into blobs with comet tails and scurried away to the east. The breeze flickered along the shore, making tough grasses nod at its coming and lifting tufts of the grey wool that had been a sheep. For the first time the woman smelled decay.

She crouched by the window and cupped a hand around one of the bars that imprisoned her.

2

Linda lived in a cathedral town, a quintessential piece of England. Her flat was over a shop in a medieval alley that linked the commercial heart of the city with its spiritual centre, the cathedral green. Turf had given way to tarmac, spirituality to business: shoppers and tourists paid heavily for the convenience of parking on the green.

Everything was crooked. The alley did not run straight: a kink prevented a clear view through. Flagstones were furrowed by centuries of shoe leather. Buildings sagged against each other. Jettied first storeys lurched forward, threatening to touch above the heads of the burdened shoppers, the dawdling tourists and the alley's few residents such as Linda.

From her kitchen, at the rear of the flat, she looked out on a slice of red-tiled roofscape, a grey slab of cathedral tower and a segment of flying buttress. It was not much of a view. It was not much of a flat either, but it was the best she had been able to do and when the time came around that she could afford better, she found herself unwilling to move.

She had married a man who was an oyster. The metaphor was forced on her during one of their holidays. They were in Ireland again, in an oyster bar again, because both were his choices again. Once the idea struck her she was stuck with it. He did not give, it was increasingly difficult to get him to open up. In the early days she had believed he was shy, and that she was one of the few people with whom he felt comfortable. Three years into the marriage she had ticked off on her fingers the friends she did not see any more, all those who had fallen away because Richard shut them out. She sensed she was next, that it was already happening.

Exclusion and evasion were making them strangers. She no longer knew who his colleagues were because he had stopped mentioning them. It was a long while since he had told her any of the day to day details of his work. If he had heard from his family, he had passed on no news. All her questions were efficiently turned aside and there was no compensating interest in what *she* did or said. She left.

The flat by the cathedral felt dark and awkward the first time she entered it. She had come from modern brickwork and picture windows, and here she was considering a future with sloping floors, undulating ceilings, and the ding of a jeweller's shop bell down below. The main attraction was the low rent, low because redecoration was overdue and because the flat was available for only three months. She took it.

She became friendly with the jeweller, a brittle old man with a big nose, who passed his days studying window shoppers deciding not to come in. Now and then he and Linda had a cup of tea together in the shop, using a glass-topped display cabinet as their table. No one was likely to disturb them. From below the willow pattern cups and saucers, a marcasite brooch that was shaped like a bow winked up and an array of gold charms, designed to bounce on a bracelet, lay stiffly undesired.

Richard sold the house where they had lived together in a town a dozen miles away. Linda received her share but she did not move. She wangled to stay on at the flat. The owner, a businessman who had bought up leases on a good number of old city centre properties, admitted that his plans for it had fallen through and he was in no hurry to take possession. She walked home content. Mr Wilkins, the jeweller, beckoned. He did not offer tea, he was busy stocktaking. She detected anxiety behind his smile. Stock-taking was not going to spring any surprises but it would force him to face up to the fact that his business was a sham. He sold hardly anything.

Linda went upstairs and did some stock-taking of her own:

Item: One failed marriage.
Item: A few thousand pounds from the sale of one suburban semi.
Item: An enjoyable job with exasperating colleagues. No, unfair. Make that *one* colleague.
Item: An average number of friends, mostly immersed in motherhood and babytalk.
Item: An untroublesome and far off family.

She caught her reflection in the mirror on the wall above the fireplace and grimaced, thinking that her other assets amounted to no more than a pleasant although not beautiful face; thick, light brown hair that she wore too long and too young; a strong, slim body; and an amenable temperament which inclined her to laziness. She felt depressingly ordinary.

For thirty-plus years it was a pathetic tally. So where had they gone, her ambitions and ideals? When had she shut her mind to the poetry she used to write? Somewhere, in a box with the books she had no room to unpack, were the little magazines where she had published. There ought also to be a tape of the poem that was read on the radio. And what about the travelling and the studying and the reaching out that she had intended? What had become of the urge to make herself busy and useful in the world?

Richard was a part of the answer but not all. She had chosen to saunter through the days in an unachieving way. It had seemed enough to have married and then enough to be divorcing, but none of that was enough for the girl she had once been. It seemed peculiar that until now she had not noticed.

She started to seek the box containing the literary magazines. Then she gave it up because poetry was not the point, it was her life she was missing.

Rusty was a witchy woman: fat, sharp nose in a yellowish face, unruly grey hair hanging over her shoulders. There was even a tooth missing, on the top right, visible whenever she smiled. She was usually eating, digestive biscuits in particular. She got crumbs on the counter and Linda swore she got crumbs in the books.

'They've found another one,' Rusty said as Linda arrived at the shop.

Another body, she meant. Gloucester, a nice cathedral city, a quintessential piece of England, and round the corner was a semi-detached house stashed with a murderer's victims.

Rusty shuddered, hair and jowls quivering. 'God, when I think . . .'

But Linda had switched off. She did not want to think about that. What was there to think? You could gape, recoil, pose answerless questions about evil and living next to it, but it did not bear thinking about.

Rusty called down the shop after her: 'Coffee's made, Linda.'

Jerome was pouring it when Linda entered the back room. He greeted her without taking his eyes off the pot.

'Good morning, Linda. Perfect timing.'

'I've been practising.' She slipped off her coat. 'Do you know,

6

this room has the smells I like most? Fresh coffee and new books.'

Jerome owned the bookshop, although customers generally assumed Rusty did. She might look a mess but she was excellent at the job, knew the trade better than any of them. Jerome had virtually bought Rusty when he bought the shop.

He was slight, mid-thirties, looked younger and was probably gay. Nobody said so and he was not camp. The gaps suggested it, particularly the reticence about his life outside shop hours. He lived over the shop, in a flat that shrank around him as stock took over one room and then another. Books were now pursuing him down the passage. They had already commandeered a yard of wallspace in the bathroom. Their progress gave Linda a nervous feeling in the pit of her stomach.

A telephone rang. Jerome let Rusty answer on the extension by the counter. She had a well-modulated voice and was good on the telephone too. He passed Linda a mug, bone china entwined with flowers. Pretty. The things he chose were. Sometimes they talked about art shows or concerts. He went, she had lapsed but read the arts pages in the newspapers instead. It was just sufficient to hold a conversation.

This morning he was quiet, they both were. Her mind was on her personal stock-taking. She had come round to blaming the dismal tally on her predisposition to laziness. Because of laziness she had sidestepped adventures. By that she meant modest ones. Big ones had not come her way. One year, for instance, she had declined shoestring travel across the globe and the next a share in a wine bar. The reasons she offered were credible: no money, no serious inclination. Behind them lay truer reasons: I don't trust myself to make a success of it, and I don't trust you. Privately, she always found it difficult to trust.

And that, she was well aware, encouraged her laziness. She had come to expect things to go awry, therefore the way to avoid disappointment was not to exert herself or to expect much of anyone else. The collapse of her marriage was not wounding, it was inevitable. In fact, she had never felt like Mrs Garvie and had dropped Richard's name as soon as they parted. Deep down she had assumed the marriage would not survive. Like the father who had left home when she was six, or the favourite uncle who had died, or the boyfriend who had switched his affections to her best friend at school just as she was beginning to believe in him, her husband had, in his own peculiar way, also let her down.

7

Although it was late in the year for resolutions, she had ended her stock-taking by making a few. Write more. Trust more. Do more.

Jerome and Linda looked up simultaneously, hearing Rusty's school-style sandals clumping down the shop and the flapping of her long, loose black dress. Rusty appeared, saying: 'That was Preston. He'll be in at half eleven.' She had a half-eaten biscuit in her hand.

Preston was a publisher's rep. He was days late because he had been filling in for a colleague who was ill and could not cover his patch on the other side of the country.

Jerome said: 'See him, will you, Rusty? I'll be out for an hour.'

He did not explain where he would be. Linda surmised he was going to a sale. Alongside the new books Jerome sold secondhand ones.

'Good stuff,' as he had explained to her when she went to work there. 'Not rubbish in pretty blocked covers, not any sort of rubbish.'

The books swallowing up the first floor of the building told the rest of the story. Early editions, beautiful books from small and fastidious presses, they were the cream of publishing. One day, Jerome would stop making appointments with the Prestons of the trade and reveal himself as a specialist dealer. That kind of business could thrive in the cathedral towns of England.

Linda sat on the corner of the desk in the back room and tapped a box with her foot. 'I'll carry on with these,' she said. It was what she had been doing the previous day until she had broken off to call on the owner of the flat and plead for her three months to be extended.

She enjoyed this part of the job: opening the boxes of new books, ticking them off against the orders, and settling them into their alphabetically correct positions along the shelves. A book on a shelf was something accomplished, completed too, except for the process of selling and that was in the customer's control, not hers. Previously, she had been a secretary and a cook but she liked the bookshop best.

Linda smoothed her hand over a sleek dust jacket, a white one with red as brilliant as fresh blood. Publishers liked that effect and believed readers did. She rubbed a slight smudge with the sleeve of her shirt and made the cover perfect. They marked too easily, these white ones. Unfairly, whenever she took down a book that was less than pristine, she blamed Rusty and her biscuit-sticky fingers. In truth, anyone's fingers did it. With care, Linda set the book on the top shelf. She was tall enough to reach with ease. Then she returned to the box for another.

On the back cover was a photograph of the author, a boyish face that brought Linda a quiver of recognition. He was very like Mark. No, he was not, nothing at all like Mark when she looked closely. Besides, she had no idea what Mark looked like now. She counted Mark among her silliest misjudgments. The college girls had vied for him and, to her amazement, he had been attracted to Linda. But she had said no, being afraid he would move swiftly on and leave her in the kind of emotional mess she preferred to sidestep. That no was one she regretted. He was a solicitor in Bath now, and whenever she read his name in the newspapers she wondered how she would have liked being the wife of a successful solicitor, and decided she would have stood it very well.

She set the book on the shelf, obscuring the face that might once have been Mark's. Mark had especially admired her hair, she remembered. And she lifted it from her shoulders with both hands and wove it into a loose plait, which was how she had worn it the term she met him and turned him down.

Jerome left and Helen came. Helen was neat, with quiet middle-class clothes and a loudish middle-class voice. She worked part-time although, like the others, she lived alone. The reason she gave was that she had an active social life to sustain. The other one, naturally, was that she did not need a full week's money. A divorce had left her comfortable, with a paid for cottage in a Cotswold village.

She started organising Linda as soon as she was through the door. 'Shouldn't you move that box? Someone might fall over it.'

Linda grinned. The shop was empty. 'I'll be finished before the lunchtime hordes descend.'

Irony never failed to escape Helen. 'I doubt there'll be that many, but have you noticed that having all these journalists around is good for business? One presumes they read while they sit in their cars staking out the House of Horror.'

A quick flick of patent leather heels and Helen hopped across the box. As she hurried down the room, she whisked a cape from her shoulders and revealed one of her short-skirted dark suits. Some days her clothes were more country than this. Linda suspected Helen was meeting one of her friends for a drink after work. Or maybe it was only a charity committee meeting in the offing.

9

Helen hung the cape behind the door in the back room and returned, brushing imaginary dust off her fingers. One of her pet grumbles was that it was impossible to keep dust down in a bookshop. Clamped under one arm she carried what appeared to be a magazine, folded open.

Linda was straightening from the box with another book in her hand when Helen stuck the magazine in front of her. Actually, it was a brochure.

'Here you are.' Helen's voice was a blend of anticipation and triumph.

Linda returned the book to the box, biting her lip while her hair swung down and hid her face. *'Damn!'* she thought. *'I didn't dream she meant it.'*

She took the brochure but before she could read anything Helen was announcing: 'Turkey.'

'Oh.'

'Yes, I know you said not, Linda, but it sounds wonderful. Do read it, I'm sure you'll be convinced.'

Linda was appalled by the idea of going on holiday with Helen. She picked over the conversation they had had earlier in the week but failed to spot anything she had said that suggested she was persuadable. In fact, she had not said much. Like most conversations with Helen, it was severely lopsided. Helen had declared she was planning a spring holiday; Linda had murmured polite interest; and Helen had tacked on an invitation to join her, a remark that sounded both casual and impulsive.

Sitting on the floor beside the box, Linda flicked through photographs of sand and sea. Turkey. Politically unsound, possibly dangerous, and a risky place for women without men. It came way down her list of good ideas. She was no keener now than she had been on Tuesday. Less, perhaps, since her evening of stock-taking. She recognised she was in need of a change but that was not the same thing as being towed across Europe by Helen.

If she went, what would they find to do that they would enjoy equally? There were no clues in the brochure. What would they talk about? Well, presumably Helen would expect to talk and rely on Linda to listen. No, it was hopeless, she could not possibly let herself be ensnared. Oh, but if it was only a week . . . No, it was *not* a week, the minimum was ten days. Anyway, she had no desire to go to Turkey and neither could she face ten days of Helen. Helen was the colleague who exasperated her.

Accompanying these negative thoughts, Linda heard the cracking of resolutions, the ones about trusting more and doing more. She cringed.

Luckily, Helen was occupied for quite some time chasing up a book. A wellknown publisher promised delivery within forty-eight hours but never met the deadline. This time the customer, a balding man with dandruff, had waited three weeks, during which he had progressed from impatience to sarcastic abuse. Seeing him approaching the door, Helen had volunteered to attend to him. She used her bossiest voice for the telephone call to the publisher. She enjoyed that part of the job.

Eventually she was free to ask Linda about Turkey. Linda sighed and squirmed and demurred. 'It's not quite what I . . . I mean, I'm not sure I'm going to take a holiday . . .'

Helen trampled the objections. 'Turkey's one of the most exciting destinations, and they say it's not completely ruined by tourism yet. Of course you need a holiday.'

The point she did not make, but let Linda understand, was that there they were, two unattached women facing the hurdle of the solitary annual holiday and what could be more convenient than for them to head for the sun in tandem?

'We'll speak again on Monday,' Helen said, accepting delay rather than refusal.

It was said in her most decisive tone. Linda felt like a fish with the hook in its flesh.

Linda bought a Sunday newspaper near the Cross and then went to a cafe where she ordered *cappuccino* and croissants. This was one of the rituals of her new single life. She enjoyed the hissing excitement of the Gaggia espresso machine, the clattering of the crockery and the dragging of the chairs as other customers came and went, and the greetings of the staff who acknowledged her status as a regular. Most of all she liked the freedom to take small actions such as this without having to justify or explain, or to persuade a reluctant partner to come along.

Three men and a woman arrived shortly after her and sat at the next table. Journalists, she gathered. They had only one topic of conversation, the story that had drawn them there. She kept her eyes on her newspaper but listened to them. The conversation proved banal. There was nothing to say they were in a privileged position, had seen whatever was to be seen, and had teased details from the policemen who were dealing with the worst of it. They might have been any group of friends mulling over the papers on a Sunday morning.

'When you think about it,' said one of the men who sat with his back to Linda, 'it could be happening all over the place. We're here because it's meant to be unique but . . .'

'No,' objected the woman. 'We're here because we're afraid it's *not* unique. If it's gone on here unnoticed for over twenty years, it could easily be happening elsewhere.'

A cadaverous man with granny glasses spoke next. 'She's right, Steve, about people being afraid. It's the "fear of crime" thing again, isn't it? Curse of the modern age and so on.'

The first man fought back. 'The circumstances are right for murders on this scale. You know, people moving around more than they did, family ties weaker, friendships more transient, homelessness . . . People expect to lose touch. If you're bumping people off, you could get away with it for years.'

'What interests me,' said the woman, 'is all those people who deliberately go missing. A false destination, a false name and they're away.'

One of the men chuckled. 'I had a week like that in Corfu once. My wife thought I was . . .'

The coffee machine erupted. Linda saw the woman talking, waving her hands to enforce a point. By the time the noise subsided, the first man was citing names: Neilson, Nilson, Sutcliffe, Young, Christie, all the multiple killers whose names sprang to mind.

Linda turned the page of her paper. A policeman emptied a wheelbarrow of soil from a cellar that was a grave. She turned another page. War, carnage, crime, dishonesty. Another page, then another until she came to the travel section. Come to Italy, it urged, forget your cares, soak up the sun and the wine, get away from it all.

What if Helen had suggested Italy, she wondered. Would she have been tempted? She drifted off into a daydream of Italy, memories of her holiday in Tuscany the previous year: lizards on old stone; tables beneath awnings; pale frescoes and bright light. She had gone with a friend from college days, Kathy. Richard would not have been enticed but in any case she made it seem purely a favour she was doing for Kathy: her friend had been let down, there was a spare ticket, and so on.

'We must do this again,' Kathy told her, over the last glass of wine on the final evening.

But they would never do it again. Kathy had another man now, a different range of interests, and a new home up north. It was her turn to be attached, Linda's to be loose.

Home after her day in the bookshop, Linda continued to dream of Italy. She began by thinking it would be good to be there and ended with a scheme to fend off Helen.

By Monday lunchtime she had acquired a brochure advertising holidays in Italy, she had asked Jerome for two weeks off work, and she had tried out the lie on Rusty. It sounded fair enough: for the second year running her friend had telephoned and invited her to Italy.

Rusty paused mid-biscuit and smiled her gap-toothed smile. 'A good thing you didn't fix anything up with Helen,' she said, and followed this with a knowing wink.

Linda wished she knew whether this was a signal that her Italian plans were an obvious fraud, or whether it was a comment on Helen's pushiness. She could hardly ask and was to regret that she did not.

Helen came in late. It was one of her days for country clothes: sweater and tweed skirt beneath a mac to keep out the wind. Before she was properly through the door she was telling Rusty what a frightful amount of time she had wasted trying to park the car. In the back room she met Linda and Jerome. Jerome was handing Linda a book.

'One for you, Linda. Take it with you, if you like.'

Linda read out the title. '*Travels in Tuscany*. Oh, are you sure, Jerome?'

'Yes, take it to Italy with you. The perfect place to read it.'

Helen hung her mac on the back of the door. She spoke over her shoulder. 'Are you going to Italy again, Linda?'

'Next week. Kathy fixed it. We talked last year about doing it again and she took me at my word.'

It was funny how the lies came tripping out. You only had to give them permission and there they were, reinventing the world. Entertained by this flight into mendacity, she did not actually notice how Helen absorbed the news that Turkey was off.

On her way home, she was forced to back out of the alley to let a party of American tourists through. A bulky man who appeared to be in charge of them blocked her way. 'Say, do you know where Cromwell Street is?'

Murder as a bonus to tourism. They would continue to come for the cathedral but from now on they would demand Cromwell Street too. Distasteful. She considered claiming to be a stranger but they would only ask someone else, so she gave directions.

The jeweller waved as she approached his window. He made her tea. 'Going to Italy?' The brochure was poking out of her bag. 'I'm taking a couple of weeks off work. From Friday.' She did not want to lie to him too so she changed the subject by making a mild joke about one of the cathedral clergy who came past the window at breakneck speed. Then they talked of other things, many other things although there was no mention of stock-taking.

The floor of her flat sloped. The chest of drawers was jacked up on pieces of wood to keep it roughly level. Even so, years of distortion made the drawers stick. With difficulty she opened the middle one and took out her photographs of Tuscany. She spread them on the dining table. Summer glowed up at her. Summer, not a wet, windy early spring which is what most of Europe was enduring. It would be a waste to go there and not have summer.

Linda lined up other objections too. She convinced herself that much as she had loved Italy in summer, she would hate it in the cold and the wet, having a poor grasp of the language and no companion to share the days.

Where, then? She had to go somewhere. She could not hide in the flat for a fortnight, and to venture out into the alley was to risk meeting Helen, who was extravagant enough to park on the cathedral green; or Jerome, who lived over the bookshop five minutes walk away.

Abruptly she gathered up the sunshiny pictures and thrust them into the drawer. Something at the back caught her eye. It was a postcard, bought in Italy. The view was of a mountainside plunging to a river. Odd, she thought, that she should have chosen this one as she did not care for heights. Turning the card over to check the name of the place, she was surprised to discover the card was not unused. It had been through the post from Sienna to England.

Then she recollected. Her cousin, Janet, and her husband had taken a villa in Tuscany for a summer, two years ago. They had all met up at a family wedding in Devon in the spring and Janet had urged Linda and Richard to visit. Later, she had sent a reminder, a postcard with a jokey cliche as a message. 'Wish you were here.'

They had not gone, of course. Richard had said he did not much like Janet's husband and anyway he was eager to revisit Connemara. He had barely glanced at the scene of the mountain dropping away to the river.

Remembering her disappointment, and annoyed with herself for not having taken up Janet's offer regardless, Linda carried the postcard through to the sitting room. Above the gas fire was a mantelpiece. She put the card there. Its economy summed up Janet, she thought: no effort spent on the message, the signature a mere initial J, and the address typed on one of those sticky labels that come on a roll. The Italian post office had entered into the spirit by stamping so meanly that the date was illegible.

Helen did not mention Turkey again nor hint at feeling rejected. Instead, she made a point of being terribly kind to Linda, which was worse. She did it in such a loud voice and so frequently that Linda felt patronised and idiotic. Rusty's winks behind Helen's back were no help either. Linda was virtually certain Rusty knew the Italian holiday was a ruse. She suspected Helen did too.

Only Jerome appeared to take it at face value. He kept on finding other relevant books among his secondhand stock and foisting them on her. He was going at it with the dedication of a truffle hunter, digging around in his upstairs hoard and emerging in triumph.

'Here you are, Linda,' he would say, thrusting the latest brown-tinged find at her. 'It's a bit tattered but it's beautifully written and the steel engravings are wonderful period pieces.'

Dog-eared triangles fell away from the corners of friable pages as she opened the books. Each time her gratitude sounded more forced than the last.

'Oh, it's lovely. Thank you, Jerome. I'll take great care of it, I promise.'

She had to carry the volumes home where she ranged them along the mantelpiece beside the postcard. All in all, it was a difficult week. On the Friday Helen, leaving early, used her sweetest voice to wish her a super holiday.

'Do promise you'll send us a postcard, Linda.'

Linda promised. Then Helen was through the door and away. Linda turned to catch Rusty's expression of gleeful malice. The woman was unnervingly like a witch.

Next morning Linda told Mr Wilkins: 'I'm playing a practical joke on my colleagues.'

There seemed no harm in confiding in the jeweller and she had

15

reached the point where she required an accomplice. He was in her flat, the first time he had come up. She had been alarmed at how slowly he had mounted the steep staircase. He was more fragile than she had suspected, the big nose seemed the sturdiest thing about him. But now he was in her best armchair, a cup of tea on the table beside him, and a postcard in his hand. It had taken her most of an evening to prepare it: steaming off Janet's sticky label and replacing it with one addressed to the bookshop, overwriting the biro message with a felt tipped pen so that it looked like her handwriting, and curling the initial J into the first letter of Linda.

'Pop it through the door on Monday week,' she suggested. 'I know it's rather quick, they'll think the first thing I did when I got there was post it, but I want it to arrive before I get back.'

He gave her an indulgent smile. 'All right, I'll play your game with you. But where will you really be, Linda?'

'I'm going to drive up to Yorkshire, and see a friend who's moved there.'

He raised an eyebrow. 'Do you have a car?'

'Oh, yes. It's not very wonderful and I don't use it much. Well, I hardly need it now I live so close to work. I keep it in a lock up garage.'

A few minutes later he put the card in the breast pocket of his suit and walked carefully downstairs. She heard the ping of the doorbell as he unlocked the shop and went in.

In the late afternoon, once it was dark, she dressed in a mackintosh with the hood up, and went down the alley and across the cathedral green. A cluster of Japanese tourists were staring up at the tower through shimmering drizzle. Inside, the choir was singing.

Linda hurried on, along a lane and across a road, until she reached the garages near the playing fields. The only people she noticed were hurrying too, heads bent because of the rain. No one saw her near the garages or driving away into the darkness.

16

3

The woman crouched at the window and cupped a hand around one of the bars that imprisoned her. Hours had passed since she imagined the boat and the man's return. She hunched there, breathing the damp salt air, afraid that if she relaxed her guard she would miss a sign.

The tide was middling now, not high and not low. Most of the time all she could hear was the panting sob of the surf, but occasionally a big white wave would come swishing in and slap against the rocks and flick spume high into the air. Then the gulls grew raucous and darted about the sky until they recovered their temper and their perch upon the rocks.

He ought to have come. He ought not to have done this to her. She chewed her lower lip and rehearsed, again, the various problems that might have detained him. The boat, first. He was not clever with boats or with engines, any number of things could have prevented him setting out from the harbour. Next, the shopping. It was too late to put all the blame on difficulty with the shopping, although that could have contributed. Then there was falling among friends. Perhaps he had met someone and been caught up in arrangements he could not break. Or, the worst, maybe his identity had been challenged. There was that possibility too.

She pictured him sneaking glances at his wristwatch and fretting about getting back to her. Of course, he would not dream she was in trouble. All he knew was that she was alone on the islet. His 'quick trip' had stretched into hour after tedious hour, which was bad enough, but he did not know she was trapped in a cell. No, a cellar. That is what she meant, a cellar. She acknowledged her slip with a faint ironic smile.

Whatever had happened, he was sure to be with her by evening. If he could not make it in the little boat, then he would hire a boatman to bring him over. There was no problem, really there wasn't.

To pep herself up she counted the good things. She was in the dry, she had ample space, fresh air, a beautiful view, and because it was so cold in the house she was wearing her jacket. In the pockets of the jacket were a few paper tissues, an almost complete roll of peppermints, and an emery board nail file. She had eaten three of the peppermints and was worrying about a fourth.

Taking one out of the packet, she held it on the flat of her hand. Her hunger was acute. She had eaten a niggardly amount the previous day and woken up famished. According to his note he had gone to the harbour village to fetch food, but she was too hungry to wait for that. She had taken a tin from the cupboard, one with the stodgiest contents. Who cared if people did not eat meatballs for breakfast? This was an emergency, anything would do.

She groaned at the memory: ransacking the kitchen for the tin-opener; searching the other rooms for it and eventually, in desperation, the cellar; and hearing the *clunk* as the door swung behind her.

She considered the peppermint. How long was it since the last one? Waves had been lapping a rock shaped like a baby whale when she popped it into her mouth. The whale was submerged now, but how long ago had it disappeared? No way of gauging that. All right, eat the peppermint.

Bending her head over her palm, she stroked the sweet with her tongue. Smooth, chalky, sugary and scented, it would fool her stomach and bring respite from grumbling emptiness.

She raised her eyes and scanned the water for a boat. If she knew when it might come she could dole out the peppermints sensibly. For a minute or so she peered at the white disc, shiny where her tongue had touched it. She spent a long time thinking before she licked it again, and longer before she resolved to stop being histrionic. She ate it.

Slowly she ate it. She held it motionless in her mouth to keep it intact as long as possible. But she felt the flow of saliva, felt the sweet dissolving, felt its sugariness trickling down her throat. Her head filled with the potent scent of peppermint. Unable to resist, she turned the disc about. Her tongue worked at eroded edges, found a thin spot. The disc broke up and the fragments dissolved, fast.

All the time, her eyes had been on the far shore and the strip of

18

water inbetween. There were no boats. She nagged at him. *'Come on, come on. Why don't you come? What can be so important that you haven't come yet?'*

Again she went over the likely reasons: a problem with the boat or the shopping; a happy meeting with an old friend or a less congenial one with someone who knew he was not who he said . . . No, they were no good. They were excuses to cover the first hour or two, they were not solid enough to be explanations for an absence of this length. The tide was coming in and the day was going.

The tide. Of course, he was waiting for the tide. Having missed one, he preferred to cross the sound when there was a good depth of water. At high tide, snagging rocks and weeds were safely out of the way. Yes, that was obviously the answer. He had come up against one problem or another and once it was sorted out he had chosen to wait for high tide.

Comforted by the thought, she moved from the window. After stretching to ease stiff limbs, she inspected her prison again. The cellar was not a neat rectangle because one wall of it was rock which bellied into the room and then sloped away upwards. At, more or less, a right angle to that wall was the one with the door. Facing the door was the window. The fourth wall was distinguished by a few old iron nails, rooted in the stone as pegs to hang things on. The pegs were empty. Low down on the rock wall, there was a shelf. Where the rock curved away, someone had straightened the line by filling in the gap with a shelf, like a deep step leading nowhere.

Except for the slab of rock, the room was plastered and had been painted white, although this was weathering away, quite severely in places. Marks on the shelf showed where things had stood. She walked over to sit on it, it was deep enough and wide enough for that although not sufficiently long to lie on. From there she could not see out of the recessed window at all. As her eyes adjusted to the gloom in that corner, she realised there was something standing on the shelf. It was a flat tin that had been parted from its lid. She fingered it and then put it back where it came from.

The discovery of the tin, which she had not noticed until then, sent her round the room seeking other unobserved details. She noted how the walls had tilted as the building settled. The one with the door was particularly odd, seeming to lean inwards. No wonder the door had swung. Although she had done so hours ago, several times, she examined the door minutely. On the other side of it lay steps up to the rest of the house, to food and warmth.

There seemed no possibility of getting herself to the other side. Where there had once been a handle, there was only a hole but this hole did not go right through the door. Something on the other side was blocking it off. She struggled to remember what the outside of the door looked like. This was difficult as she had always seen it jacked open. He had used a stone for that.

What, then, had gone wrong? There was no stone in the room with her. Just as she had entered she heard the whoosh of movement and the door was swinging rapidly in behind her. If she had been quick enough . . . But no, it had been too sudden and it was such a heavy door, she'd had no chance of stopping it. The odd thing was she had previously been in the cellar without mishap, and he had been down there a number of times. It was the worst possible luck that the day she was alone was the day the door slammed.

She returned to the window. Water was swilling over a group of rocks that were one of her measuring points. Stone was concealed but frothing water gave it away. Soon, though, it was going to be safe and he would know it was time to leave the harbour. It was simply a matter of waiting for nature to make it convenient, and nature could not be hurried. She was schooling herself in patience.

She filed her fingernails, giving them the attention she seldom spared them. Then she smoothed her hair and made a loose plait of it, and when it felt uneven, she did it again until she got it right. She had time.

Picking over the words of his note, she pictured it lying on the kitchen table, beside the unopened tin of meatballs. It read: 'I'm making a quick trip while you sleep.' Or something like that. She had recited it so often she was remembering the remembering. At one stage she believed he had specifically mentioned shopping, but now she thought not. Why should he? She understood where he had gone and what was needed. Sneaking off before she was awake was a smart way of avoiding taking her with him, and he had been aware she was desperate to get over to the harbour. But that was another matter and did not explain this awful delay.

Waiting. So much of everyone's life was wasted in waiting, she thought. Children waited for birthdays and Christmases, long before they had a concept of time passing in a day by day, month by month progression. She catalogued dreary waits in post office queues before the system was streamlined; in the schoolyard until her mother collected her; in the wind and the cold while her husband – nearly her ex-husband – had his fill of ancient ruins; waiting on telephone lines that played terrible music and turned an inconvenience into a torment; for appointments and friends and lovers, waiting in disgruntled resignation or happy anticipation. All that waiting.

'How do I categorise this wait?' she wondered. He was a lover she no longer wanted and he was the only person who knew where she was. With a flicker of humour she invented a new category: frantic waiting. She decided to share the thought with him later, once they were on the main island. Perhaps he would relish the bitter irony of saving her only to have her reject him.

The wind turned and the sour smell of the dead sheep wafted into the cellar. A couple of black-backed gulls were stabbing at it but most of the birds in her view were picking over the sandy expanse the tide was reclaiming. They fluttered near the surf, with the anxiety of last minute shoppers. On the rocks nearest the shore, one was smashing shellfish. He lifted them in his beak, rose into the air, let them fall, dropped down to examine his work, repeated as necessary, and gradually and efficiently destroyed them.

As the tide rose, daylight faded. Electric lights were switched on in houses across the water. A dark creature slunk along the beach and nuzzled the carcase of the sheep. Water that had been the colour of gunmetal all day changed subtly, and before long the mountains, the shore and finally the sea were enveloped in a gauzy mist.

With a rush of self-pity she realised he would not leave the harbour that day. She cursed him and cried, and vowed not to sleep in case the mist cleared and he raced to rescue her after all. And then she dozed anyway.

Inevitably, her dreams were of food, and also of tea in thick white cups too heavy to lift when brimming. They forced her to bend her head over them and sip, while the steam tickled her face and made her skin slippery. When she had sipped a half inch and could try out her strength at cup lifting, a teapot loomed over her, a hand drew her back, the spout was lowered and the level in her cup was raised to the rim. 'An excess of kindness,' said a voice in her dream. It was not her voice, or at least she did not think so, although there was no one else in the dream with her, except for the presence holding the teapot. Again she sipped, again she was drawn back and the cup refilled. In the magical way of dreams, no milk jug or bottle appeared and yet the flavour of the tea was constant.

Waking, she worried that it had not been a dream at all but a trick of the mind like the time she spotted the boat. She hauled herself up from the floor and peered out.

A breeze was tearing the mist into wisps and throwing them about, giving her glimpses of the other shore. She saw a glow of light from a house on the hillside. As she watched, it was extinguished, leaving her feeling more alone.

A while later she heard a boat engine, or dared to believe she did. She grabbed at the bars with both hands, crammed herself into the recess, ignoring the discomfort in her bruised shoulder. Rags of mist were blowing down the channel so her view was patchy and unclear. The engine grew weaker, fading to nothing.

Too weary for arguments with God or for railing against the man who did not come, she slumped on her knees in front of the window. She felt adrift, as though she were the one on a turbulent journey. Her hand reached for one of the bars, something strong and reliable to cling to. In a moment, without knowing it, she began to suck the thumb of her free hand. She stayed there and waited for the dawn.

4

The wipers flumped across the screen leaving an arc of shining black. There was a road with a seam of glittering Cat's-eyes, bowing shapes of trees, and the occasional country pub with coloured fairy lights around a porch. Much of the time there was nothing to see but the road.

Linda was exhilarated by this journey into oblivion. She felt free, not unlike the day she had moved into the flat in the alley, shut the door behind her and turned the key. There had been no need for her to be locked in but she wanted a sense of possession, individuality, aloneness. It was the same now in the car: the vehicle defined her and she controlled it. She could do anything she liked.

She believed this until she arrived at the hotel. Several years ago she had gone to a friend's wedding reception held there and it stuck in her mind as a beautiful house in an almost secret setting. Quite small, with perhaps fewer than a dozen rooms, it had an air of old-fashioned comfort. Her only firm plan for the holiday was that on the first evening she would drive no further than this hotel.

It was full. A company had booked it for a weekend conference.

The manageress, an exopthalmic woman with several chins, offered to telephone other hotels and find a room for her but Linda said no.

'Well, let me write two or three addresses down for you,' the woman said, determined to be helpful.

The first Linda came to looked big and brash in its car park floodlights. She did not slow the car. The second was a mile away from the main road and she decided not to turn off. Before she reached the third she spotted a pretty black and white house with a B and B sign by its hedge. She stayed there.

The room was quaint and the plumbing quainter. Across the road was a pub where she ate supper, a microwaved pie and a mound of

23

chips jostling a lettuce leaf and half a tomato off the plate. The coffee had stewed so long that it tasted like poisoned licorice. There was a television set to watch, and to listen to even if you did not choose to watch. She would have sworn that the three other people in the bar did not once take their eyes from the screen, not so much as look her over as she entered.

Birds woke her in the morning. She threw off the pastel-patterned duvet and stood at her window. No rain but the landscape gleamed, especially the ivy that seemed to knit together the wonky garden wall. Daffodils trumpeted spring. She ran a lukewarm shower and went down to a lavish breakfast. As the room was cheap, she paid in cash. Then she nosed her car out from its hiding place behind the hedge and she was on her way.

She meandered through the border country, 'that land of unstable identity' as the Welsh writer Dorothy Edwards called it. After Sunday lunch in a pub, she stood on a windy ridge on Offa's Dyke, the great demarcation line between the free Britons of the Welsh mountains and the Anglo-Saxons of the kingdom of Mercia.

All day she inspected archaeological sites and famous views. There were few people around once the smattering of churchgoers had gone home from morning service. Occasionally, she encountered parties of stick-clutching walkers, forced on to a stretch of road linking the muddy footpaths they preferred. Or she passed weekend riders, two abreast in conversation, and cross when drivers misunderstood gesticulation for hand signals. But the weather had not encouraged many people to come out. After the sunny start the day had grown dull and cold.

Linda parked her car beneath trees on a hilltop and felt it buffeted by wind rushing up the scarp from the broad valley. She slotted a tape into the player. A BBC programme presenter said a few words and then an actress read Linda's poem. It was the first time she had listened to it since digging the tape out of a box beneath her bed. She tingled with recognition, pride almost, but after hearing it she grew critical. The poem was not perfect, they hardly ever were. She wondered about swapping a word, altering a phrase.

On a blank page in her diary she made a note of possible changes. Immediately she realised that her replacement word would not do, not at all, because it was similar to one in the first stanza. It would be an unwarranted distraction, not an enhancing repetition. She cancelled her note with a scribble and closed the diary. Tomorrow, when the shops opened, she was going to buy a notebook and use this strange, cold, solitary journey to revive her poetry. Although she did not yet have a line for a new poem, she sensed that before long she would.

Another night, another bed and breakfast. The shower was hotter and more energetic, the breakfast was meaner. Round the back of the house a gutter hung loose and tiles had slipped. The girl who served breakfast wore a woolly so worn at the wrist that no yarn anchored the lines of stitches and the garment was thinly disappearing. A farmworker led a herd of cows up the lane as Linda looked down from her bedroom. The animals' breath was steam. When they rounded the bend in the lane, and were out of her sight, steam seemed to issue from the hedgerow instead and bowl along the top of it.

In the distance were the tall chimneys of an industrial estate on the edge of a town. She headed that way, bought her notebook, mooched around Monday morning clothes shops with half-stocked rails, and called in at the library where the tourist information centre was housed. The countryside had put up a Closed sign: it was the wrong month to be taking a drifting kind of holiday. Stately homes and other tourist attractions were not ready for visitors.

Sifting through brochures, she picked a country hotel in lovely wooded grounds and made a booking. Rain splashed down all the way there. She admitted that she hated the weather and that, so far, every aspect of the holiday had been a disappointment. Worst of all, she was lonely. She missed having someone to laugh with and share with. The exciting solitude of her first evening had dispelled.

Linda swung into the hotel entrance, too fast, spraying gravel from the drive. From the first moment the place felt right. There was old wood and flowery fabrics, a nice example of the English country house style. She decided to nestle down there until the weather changed for the better. Early that evening she shut herself in her room and began work on a poem. At once there was a problem. The bottle of ink she had brought appeared to be about a fifth full but what was left turned out to be a deceptive stain on the glass. She treated the setback as a lesson in not being fussy about the tools she used, put aside her fountain pen and set to work with a biro.

The following day she walked in borrowed wellingtons among the trees, alone except for fugitive birds. Doubtful about one line of the poem, she wrote down an alternative. By evening she had a whole verse.

The achievement gave her a lift. Happy, she was tired too. She had forgotten how the sort of concentration she needed to write could drain her of physical and mental energy. It had been so long since the last poem. Knowing she would write no more that day, she took a book to read by the log fire downstairs. The hotel was silent. She supposed it possible she was the only midweek guest but she had been reading for less than fifteen minutes when she was interrupted. That is how she met him.

There was nothing memorable about him. If she had been pressed to say what he seemed like she would have reached for words like average and ordinary. His opening conversation was unexceptional too.

'Good to see a real old fashioned log fire, isn't it?'

That way he immediately got her to say 'Yes.'

'It's a pity so many pubs and hotels have gone over to stoves. They're attractive, but there's nothing to equal a good log fire.'

Rather than repeat the yes, she gave an appreciative murmur and bent her head to her book.

And then he had settled into the chair on the other side of the fire, taken up a magazine and browsed, and left her alone. She found it easy to ignore him. He was dull, he was nothing.

The important meeting came the following day. As she was not clear how to go on with the poem, she took a break from it and drove to a hillfort four miles away. To begin with, the track from the road was like a sunken lane through a wood. A short way in, it began to twist up the hill and soon she left the trees behind. The path was steep and slippery with mud. Also, stones had washed loose. Unkempt sheep trotted away at her approach. She stopped to catch her breath and saw great clouds rolling across from the east and casting dark splodges on sunlit hills. Shading her eyes, she sought out distant landmarks and the . . .

A car? Head inclined she listened but the droning had stopped. Linda climbed again.

Standing within the enclosure of the fort she missed Richard. He carried in his head a plan of these places, knew what all the banks and ditches indicated. She could only take a sentimental view of tumbled defences and mouldering remnants. Richard knew the value of hornworks, baffles and guard chambers. His face always used to brighten when he drew close to anything ancient and remote from the present day. She regretted not paying heed as he dragged her around the prehistory of Ireland, the ruined past of Wales, and all those out of the way spots where the spirits of ancestors roamed. Her excuse was that they were windswept and inclement places, and what had crowded her mind were feelings of discomfort, coldness and disinclination to linger.

After a brisk prowl along the ramparts, her hair streaming behind her like a flag in a breeze, she started down the track. This was worse than ascending. She stumbled and clutched at stone, or skimmed the palm of her glove along a wall of mud. As the path widened out, a loose stone spun downhill at the touch of her foot and she found herself running after it, too fast, unbalanced, out of control. The bend ahead of her was sharp. She slammed into a bank where tender greening twigs and fragile flowers were forcing through last year's dead weeds.

Just in time she prevented herself pushing the hair back from her face with mud-matted gloves. Her jacket and jeans were daubed with wet earth, the knee of one trouser leg stuck to her skin. She groaned. She had never trusted the outdoors. It was messy, difficult and best avoided.

Rounding another bend she was startled to see a red car slewed across her path. For a second she supposed it belonged to the owner of the sheep, but then rejected the idea as anyone familiar with the area would be aware the track was unsuitable for vehicles. Then the man stepped out of the trees on the far side of the car, saying: 'Oh, it's you! Hello again.'

Linda forgot about the state of her gloves and pushed the hair off her face. 'Are you stuck?'

He seemed a bit flustered, and he was windswept too. She thought him more attractive for being less neat.

He said: 'I skidded. I was trying to drive up.'

'You can't, it gets really narrow.' She reached the car and stopped. She had to unless she wanted to squash herself into the bank to squeeze behind it.

He spoke to her over the car roof. 'If I try and straighten it up, would you watch I don't clout the banks?'

'Yes, of course.' She checked the alignment of the wheels. The car had come to rest at an acute angle across the track, its offside headlamp touching the bank and its front wheels turned to the offside. He had tried to drive into the skid, the way one was taught to, and had swung the steering wheel hard to the right. Unluckily, there was no room for such a manoeuvre.

He was talking again, asking her to mind the back end because he was going to reverse as far as he could.

He eased the vehicle a fraction. 'How are we doing?'

'OK. You have another three inches.'

He moved it three inches. She told him to stop. He pulled on the handbrake and got out to see for himself.

Linda said: 'Before you move again, change the lock on your front wheels, hard left.'

With careful handling he ought to have been able to get the car straight but to her surprise, he did not keep the lock tight when he moved forward and so the car pulled into the side.

He got out again and walked to the front and then the rear, grunting disappointment. Then: 'Look . . . er . . . sorry, I don't know your name.'

'Linda.'

'I'm Tom Hoby. Look, Linda, can you shout out when I'm as close as I can get? I'm going to use every inch I can squeeze out of this.'

She bit her tongue to prevent herself offering to do it for him. To her the manoeuvres were obvious, but shunting cars involved principles that some people grasped straight off while others remained forever confused. She pigeon-holed Mr Hoby among the confused.

She liked his name, the ring of the two words together. Tom Hoby. It was a nice name, a solid and jolly English name. Words mattered to her. Names were crucial, even though her own name was inappropriate: Linda for beauty, Conway for a town she had never seen. She was a lover of words or, at least, she was swayed by them.

He ran the car back, pressed the bumper into the bank, tugged the steering wheel round and, once again, began to go wrong. She banged on the car roof.

'No, you need to keep the lock tight.'

He gave a self-mocking laugh. 'Oh, yes. I see what you mean.' Then he gripped the wheel and made the car move away from the bank, straightening it until it was lined up on the track and facing her.

She tendered the next bit of help. 'If you like, I'll walk down ahead and guide you through the bends.'

He reversed slowly after her. There was mud, a gritty surface, a hole or two, and several awkward bends. He reversed slowly after her. Now and then she paused, waving him away from obstacles. A downdraught from the hill wafted exhaust fumes over her, and she felt relieved when they reached the straight run to the roadway.

'You're all right now,' she said, perched on a rock that jutted from the bank beside the car.

He grinned up at her, making the joking offer of a lift to her car parked a few hundred yards away in the layby.

'No thanks,' she said, laughing, 'I prefer cars that go forward and stay on the road.'

When he had reversed as far as the road, he swung right, disappeared for a moment and then shot across the entrance to the track, moving away fast.

A minute later, reaching the junction herself, she automatically looked the way the red car had gone. Something teased at her but she could not pinpoint it. As she opened her car door, a few spots of rain spattered the windscreen. There were puddles in the layby and tyre tracks. The something continued to niggle.

Back at the hotel, early in the afternoon, she washed mud from her face, changed her clothes and, using her dressing table as a desk, she worked on the first verse of her new poem. The previous evening's satisfaction was giving way to criticism. There was a phrase that jarred and a line that overnight had grown clumsy. She struggled to smooth, improve, and attain her best.

It was demanding but rewarding. By the time she went downstairs to supper she was feeling pleased with herself, for her effort as much as her achievement. Tom Hoby was sitting by the fire.

'I must thank you,' he began.

'You did, more than adequately.' She was thinking he had made himself less appealing now he had washed his hair and combed it flat. He was back to being Mr Very Ordinary. And she wondered whether anyone, any woman that is, had ever done what she wanted to do, ruffle his hair and tell him how much better that looked.

'No, I'm going to buy you a drink,' he was saying. 'If it weren't for you, I'd still be wedged up that damned lane.'

She declined but he was determined to be grateful and they rapidly reached the point where she would look mean spirited if she continued to refuse him. So they sat by the fire drinking wine and comparing notes on the comfortlessness of the English countryside in winter. It was a fancy way of talking about the weather, as strangers usually do.

Fortunately, she found him very easy, and a glass of wine beside

29

the fire led to them sharing a table for supper. There were two other guests in the dining room, a couple of businessmen who talked jargon – cookie cutter technology and leading edge featured prominently – in voices that increased in volume as more and more drinks were downed.

Although he asked where her home was, Linda did not mention Gloucester to Tom because to do so would spark off a discussion of the House of Horror. Instead she said Bristol, and felt lucky when he said he did not know it. He lived in London.

She drew a picture in her mind: a terrace house, the lower part white stucco and the rest London brick; three door bells and an entryphone; a flat at the top with an angled ceiling; and a view across slate roofs to the sharpened-pencil outline of Canary Wharf tower. A tiny flat, it was central but too small for his children who came to visit every other weekend. She saw him walking down the terrace with them, taking them to the Natural History Museum or the Science Museum.

He had not told her any of that but it was what men did and he was older than her, nearer forty, the sort of age to be living that kind of life. She could not remember who actually occupied the flat she was using for this piece of make-believe. Perhaps it was not someone she knew at all, merely a flat she had seen on television. Memories of life and of television regularly became scrambled.

The businessmen were discussing whether to order coffee or whether coffee was likely to ruin a good night's sleep in which case they would be wiser to have more brandy. The waiter waited, a patient half smile on his face. As he turned away to fetch the brandy, the smile broadened.

'I used to do that,' Tom said.

'Waiting?' She knew he did not mean that but she could imagine him as a waiter, blending unobtrusively into the background.

'Sales rep. OK, waiting too but that was only a holiday job.'

'What did you sell?'

'Not much. That's why I gave it up.'

He shared the last of the wine between their glasses. Then: 'After that I had my own company. Computerware.'

She pictured the unreliable creditors, the unpaid bills, the winding up. The bankruptcy? No, she wiped out the image of the bankruptcy court.

'What now?' she asked him.

'Like you, Linda, I'm taking time out.'

She had not mentioned the bookshop, only the spell away from work. She said: 'I hoped to wander through England, enjoy it and enjoy the enjoying of it. But what happens? Rotten weather.'

'If the weather bothers you, why didn't you go abroad?'

It was on the tip of her tongue to tell him. The wine was tempting her to but she held back. 'Abroad is having rotten weather too. A lot of it is, anyway.'

She took another sip. 'I suppose I was thinking of those American novels or films where people jump in their cars and drive for days, any direction they choose. And if they don't like it when they get there, they just change direction and carry on driving. It's so huge, there's all that freedom, they can do it. But here . . .'

'By the time you're in top gear you're in sight of the sea again.'

He was watching her over the rim of his glass. His attention encouraged her to elaborate.

She said: 'And it's not simply a problem of geography. Over there, they achieve a sense of escape. Space, yes, but crossing state lines and seeing the changing cultures gives an impression of having gone further than in reality. What we have is so cramped, so minimal. You know, they can drive a thousand miles without leaving the USA. If we do it, we're in, say, the south of Spain.'

As she finished her wine he said: 'Scotland, Linda. You could find space there.'

She admitted she had not been there apart from one visit to the Edinburgh festival. They agreed that did not count. She was picturing Scotland though, from television scenes: rain-lashed islands; misty mountains and soggy sheep; grouse moors and grouse; whisky and woollies; that kind of thing. The way Tom talked, he knew it fairly well.

'You can be alone up there,' he said, having misunderstood her.

The businessmen exploded in laughter and the atmosphere changed. Linda began to wind the conversation down, say what a pleasant evening it had been, and say goodnight.

A while later, drawing the curtains in her room, she noticed the red car parked below. She frowned as she jerked the curtains across. Something was still bothering her.

'It doesn't matter,' she thought. *'He'll drive away in the morning and I won't have to see him again.'*

That gave her a twinge of regret, because he had been good company at a time when she was lonely and because it was a rare luxury for her to be paid so much attention.

He had said he was going to call on a man, Stevens, a few miles away and then travel north. When she had been vague about her own plans, saying she would wait and see what the weather was like, he had mentioned a local country house that opened one afternoon a week, all year round, for visitors to ogle its beamed ceilings and buy teatowels and pots of dubious jam. Ironical, she had promised to buy her holiday souvenirs there.

The red car was gone when she opened her curtains next morning but she was not truly sorry to have missed him. They had said their thanks and their goodbyes and there was nothing to be gained from meeting up again. And yet they did.

'Teatowels or jam?' he asked, surprising her in the tea room at the country house.

'Some of each,' she admitted, removing the carrier bag from the table and making room. She was laughing with pleasure at seeing him. A minute ago she had been feeling lonely and here he was to cheer her up. 'I thought you'd be miles away by now. What happened?'

'Oh, there was a mix up. Stevens wasn't there so I've fixed another appointment for tomorrow.'

Close to the gates of the country house there was a flower shop. Fresh flowers, tasteful arrangements of dried flowers, potted plants, it sold them all. Tom and Linda had to walk past it on their way to the car park and she lingered to admire the profusion, such a spectacle in the drab days of early spring. This was a mistake because he promptly offered to buy her something. She remembered his pressure when he insisted on buying her a drink and was afraid of a repetition, but fortunately she had a perfect excuse to hand.

'But I'm travelling. They'd be wasted.'

'Oh yes, I hadn't thought.'

In the window was a sheet of grey slate engraved with a verse. 'Now if they sold those,' she said, knowing they did not because the plaque was for display only, 'I'd find it hard to resist.'

His breath steamed the pane as he read the lines. Then: 'Who's Mag Mell of the many flowers?'

Linda failed to suppress a giggle. 'It's not a woman, it's a place. A mythical one anyway.'

She glanced up at the fascia board. 'See? It's the name of the shop. It's from a Celtic legend and it means the Plain of Delight.'

'This plain, it was full of flowers, was it?'

'Certainly. Celtic legends are very beautiful.'

She frowned, trying to remember precisely. 'I'm almost sure it was actually the sea but one of the characters perceived it as a plain covered with flowers.'

'Well, *I* still see it as a woman. No, a witch. Mag is rather bewitching, don't you think? She's a beautiful witch.'

And that was when he began to call her Mag which stuck and before long evolved into Maggie.

Over supper that evening, he said: 'Look, why don't you come with me tomorrow? It's a pretty town and you could potter about while I see Stevens, and then we could have lunch.'

He coaxed her into it. She assumed he would be driving up north straight after the meeting but when she was about to get into her car next morning to follow him to the pretty town, he said there was no need to take two cars because he needed to return to the hotel. She travelled with him.

Gradually he came to be there.

'We ought to go to Scotland,' he said.

'No, too far.' She flicked her indicator on and swung out to pass a parked delivery van.

'We could have been there in the time that's passed since you started saying that.'

'I'm not going.'

He shrugged. 'OK.'

There was a tape projecting from the tape player on the dashboard. He slid it in, saying: 'I know about your taste in holidays, Linda. Now let's see about your taste in music.'

But he did not get music. A BBC presenter announced Linda's poem and an actress began to read it.

He swivelled in his seat to look at her. 'Linda Conway. Hey, that's you.'

She reached out to switch off the machine. He caught her hand. Wriggling to free herself, she protested: 'Mind, there's a bend coming up.'

He continued to hold her hand, right up until the moment when the road curved. Then he let her pull free.

'You're crazy!' she said, swinging the steering wheel, recovering.

He picked up her recorded words and teased her with them. 'That description could be Scotland, you know.'

Then he plucked out the tape and reinserted it so that the poem was played right through. He listened without interruption. After that, silence. Linda gave him a sideways look.

'Better get it over,' she thought. *'People often don't know how to respond to a poem, not in words and especially not to the author.'*

Aloud she said, in comic challenge: 'Well?'

'That bit about the sheen on the water.'

'What about it?'

'I don't understand it.'

'Oh, it's about childhood. Or perhaps old age.'

'Don't you know?'

'You can choose.'

'But you, what did you choose?'

'Childhood came first, the other meaning came later. Now I see them both. They aren't contradictory, are they?'

He said no but he said it doubtfully.

She tried again. 'When I was writing it I was thinking about a phase of innocence or lack of responsibility. Basically, the poem is about trusting oneself to life. I believed . . .'

Her explanation trailed away. He was taking a map from the shelf, not interested in what she had to say. It surprised her how annoying this was, to have her work dismissed because of one difficult line, and to have her explanation disregarded in favour of map-reading.

'Go left at the junction,' he said.

She choked back her ill humour and said yes. Her compliance irritated her and she accused herself of behaving with uncharacteristic recklessness. *'What do you think you're doing, trailing around England with a strange man who bores you with computer talk and doesn't understand poetry?'* At this moment it did not seem a good enough reply to mutter to herself about resolutions and trust.

One thing had led to another. The red car had developed a fault and he left it at a garage to await a new part. They had begun to travel together and to sleep together. Perhaps if he had asked her outright she would have said no, but there was a taking-it-for-granted side to Tom, a confidence that he understood her feelings and was free to act for her. One evening he booked a double room, a double bed, and she did not object. She was amused, and relieved too because his cheek prevented her indulging in one of her private wrangles about whether to say yes or no. She would have wanted to say yes, but might well have said no.

So she lay in bed in the moonlight that first night with him and felt his strong, soft, gentle hands moving over her breasts, parting

her thighs, and she stopped herself thinking of past or future anything but the considerable pleasures of the moment. No one h made love to her in a long while. She had not realised how m she had missed it.

The next morning he had brushed her hair, while she stood na in front of the mirror.

'You have the hair of a Celtic goddess,' he said, making i out. 'The Greeks and the Romans tamed theirs and curled i the Celts wore it long and free.'

'Perhaps the Celts forgot to invent the hairdresser,' she j but secretly she was pleased.

'Have you always worn it like this?'

'Forever.' She meant ever since her teens when another man she ought to have risked caring for, had admired it.

In the car, talking about her poem, Tom folded the n explained his difficulty with some of her lines. 'What I was t was what Eliot said about words. You know, somethir writers being doomed to failure because by the time the words right, they no longer want to say whatever it was.'

This caught her off guard. She groped for the exact was ashamed to discover she had never known it. How o should. Or perhaps not. Perhaps she was wrong to write a gadget man, keener on technology than art. It crosse that he might be playing with her when he started on puters, knowing the subject bored her. Like most wom sidered them tools, ranked alongside the vacuum clea washing machine. Like most men he did not.

Glancing across she caught the glint of mischief in waited for her to tidy up her reply. His name was red-cheeked farmer with honest eyes and roughened was a more subtle creature than that. She could not was. Finding out was part of the fun of being with h

'Left here, you said?' Checking the direction at th ducked the reply.

Because they were new to each other they talke a trick of making her do the talking, and winkling mation out of her. She did not confess all, she kept about coming from Bristol. Italy came up over lu

His eyes narrowed. 'Italy?'

'Yes. It's quite clever, I've actually arranged f card to be delivered to the bookshop.'

'Won't they notice the lack of a suntan when you go back?'

'No more than if I'd been to Tuscany this week.'

He shook his head, bewildered by her audacity. 'So only one person knows where you are?'

'And Mr Wilkins only knows I didn't set off for Italy.'

Her words triggered a memory. *What interests me is all those people who deliberately go missing. A false destination, a false name and they're away . . .* After a moment's puzzlement, she remembered who had spoken those words: the woman journalist in the Sunday morning cafe in Gloucester.

'Well.' Tom regarded her with renewed interest. She felt uncomfortable, afraid he was liking her less now that he knew her capable of such unkind deception. Already she wished she had not told him, or at least had sounded less self-congratulatory. Linda rallied by thinking that it was safe to assume he was also deceiving someone, a wife or a lover who believed him to be elsewhere instead of mooching around with a strange woman.

When he next spoke he made one of those hops that she found unsettling. One usually knew, roughly, what the other person was thinking about once a conversation was under way, but with him she did not.

'Tell me about your mother and the teapots.'

'The teapots? Well, as I said yesterday, she collects them. Several dozen by now, I should think. It started when we moved into a house where the previous owners had left a pine dresser.'

'Just left it?'

'Our theory was it had become impossible to remove it after they'd built an extension on the kitchen. The angle from the old back door to the new one made it out of the question. Anyway, my mother was fond of the dresser and decided she wanted teapots all along one of the shelves. Now they're everywhere. Staffordshire, Royal Worcester, Minton . . .'

'Originals or repro?'

'Mixed but a lot of them are good.'

He put on what she thought of as his wicked look. 'Gosh, does that mean I'm speaking to a teapot heiress?'

'The appalling thing is, I think you might be. But at the moment she's alive and well and taking an extended holiday in Madeira. Apparently there are cheap deals for old age pensioners.'

'Do *you* collect anything?'

'No, I lack the collector's instinct.' She skipped saying it was just

36

as well because she had left her modern house with the picture windows and moved into a crooked flat with no room to unpack all her books. 'What about you? Is there a museum of computers burgeoning in your cellar?'

'People,' he said. 'I collect people.'

She could understand that. It was something she did herself, filing away interesting people who stimulated her imagination and might one day surface in her writing. The day she met Rusty, for instance, she had noted down the hag-like figure with the long black clothes, flying grey hair and acute intelligence. Rusty was too good to miss. Collecting people was a respectable hobby, whether you intended to write about them or merely to enjoy their variety.

Linda asked what he had in his family background to equal an intemperate teapot collector.

'Nothing like that,' he said.

Then he told her stories about his childhood: a widowed mother who was a teacher, tougher on her own children than on her pupils. He had slunk away from the house to play on boats. They lived in a seaside town.

'There was a rock,' he said, 'out in the bay. I used to think if I could go there, it would be all right. Mum couldn't row so she couldn't follow me. Daft, the way kids think.'

'Did you try it?'

'No, it was only dreaming.'

His stories made her feel tender towards him, to the little boy he used to be. They were all like that, half-stories, the might have beens that never turned into adventures or escapes or turn-your-life-around opportunities. But that was normal, that was what children suffered, and it was the only trouble that time literally did cure.

He offered these stories as amusing anecdotes, although she found them sad. Between his words he was telling of disappointments.

Linda retained her mental pictures of his London flat but they were growing less vivid. He claimed neither ex-wife nor children, therefore the shot of him walking down the terrace on his way to the Science Museum was irrelevant. Once, he mentioned 'the people upstairs' which proved she was also wrong about his attic ceiling and his long views. She thought he said he lived south of the Thames but another day he mentioned Fulham so she realised she had mis-understood.

Tom was extraordinary, she thought. He was drawing her out, making her say things she did not know she believed until she said them, and showing her aspects of herself she had not known existed. While he was doing it, he was leading her into an escapade and she was not holding back. He encouraged her and she wanted to go on. Quite unusually, she felt free to trust.

When she attempted to say something of this to him, he became embarrassed and switched to a different subject. She felt foolish not to have guessed he would shy away from anything that smacked of emotional dependency. Although that was not what she meant, he had obviously taken it that way. He virtually confirmed this when, hours later, he made a remark about trust.

'It's not enough to trust other people. The key is to trust yourself.'

Sometimes he frightened her.

He frightened her the day they walked along the cliffs.

She watched his retreating back, Tom growing smaller and more remote with every step. How could he be so steady, so nerveless, so oblivious to her? Again she tried to scream, but fear had wrung the breath from her body. Craving help, she had lost the means to beg for it.

Her right hand, the one that clenched the grass, was in agony with cramp, its muscles exerting such pressure that it had locked. She had hooked her fingers through the strands, pretending extra effort made her safer. The tuft shifted a fraction as some of the roots worked loose.

Linda looked down. The world became unfocused, then hideously clear. Clumps of sea thrift, half way down the cliff, were delineated with an artist's sharp line. The same precise hand had sketched the details of the jagged rocks at the bottom.

Below, the bay was a living presence drawing her to it. Gulls, white-backed projectiles, twirled down to the foamy water. She shut her eyes. Pain spread from her hand up to her shoulder. For the rest, she was numb. She had legs and feet, and in some indefinable spot she had willpower which she understood ought to be guiding her to safety.

But it was futile to reason because her mind had lost control of her will minutes ago, around the time Tom had negligently outpaced her. She had seen the path behind him become scree and she had seen the scree fall.

He turned at last. 'Come on.'

He spoke in that chivvying tone she had caught once in a while when she had lingered for what he considered no good reason.

She appealed to him with her terrified eyes. At once he started back. Relief flooded through her as she anticipated his strong arm plucking her from danger, but after a few steps he came to a halt. He called across.

'What's the matter?'

She moistened her lips with her tongue but her words were still dried up. She stared back at him.

It struck her that he was showing off his bravery, perched on the lip of the bay, arms akimbo. Through each arm she saw a wedge of blowy sky framed by the maroon of his sweater.

'Oh, come on, Linda. It's safe enough.' And when she did not respond he proved it with: 'I did it, didn't I?'

'Yes,' she thought, 'you did. But you didn't see the path crumble beneath your weight, or the scree spinning out into the void, or the slithery surface you created for me to tread on.'

And then pain filled her whole body. There was no part of her that was not punished by it. She was trembling, swaying. Below her the cliff face and the eager water moved in untidy rhythm. Ahead the sky rocked.

He shouted then. 'For God's sake, hold on.'

He hurried to her, a hand held out long before it was of any use. His face showed concern but not fear. All the urgency was in his approach and that outstretched hand.

As he came forward, so the path disintegrated, a handful here and a handful there, like dirt thrown by mourners into an open grave.

She sensed herself sinking, uncertain whether it was actual physical movement or a trick of her mind, a metaphor for imminent collapse. Then her right arm jerked towards her, closing the slight gap between body and limb. Some of the grass had torn free. A quarter, perhaps a third of it, had been wrenched away. She watched her hand clutching blades that were no longer attached to anything. Below a gull mewed, a thin cry that gave sound to the scream trapped within her.

She lurched her body round until her left hand could scrabble for a handhold too. There was no grass within its reach, erosion had taken place too recently for anything to have colonised the bare earth. Her fingers slid around a stone, a small projection on the dusty surface. Earth went grittily under her fingernails. Roughness scraped the heel of her hand. And the stone she was relying on came free in a shower of powdery soil.

39

Yet she could not let it go. To drop it was to have a free hand flailing in space and, irrationally, she could not bear that. So she leaned into the earth bank and pressed the stone against the patch of soil it had come from. With her right hand she struggled to keep hold of what remained of the tuft of grass. Her right cheek was flattened against earth. Her eyes were closed.

When he reached her she was rigid. A chill sweat soaked her. She was wracked with nausea.

'Come on,' he said, his hand closing on her elbow.

She could not move. Again he urged her. 'Come on, it's all right.'

In her head there was a torrent of objection. *'But you said that earlier, didn't you? Before we started out along the path, you promised it was all right, that it wasn't like this, that the path was sound and safe and not too near the edge. You* promised *and look what's happened.'*

All she said, in a thick and unfamiliar voice, was: 'My legs. They won't move.'

'They will if you tell them to, Linda. Of course they will. But you've got to tell them.'

She thought: *'He sounds like a parent with a reluctant child.'* But she did not mind that, as long as he did not go away and leave her again.

She started to speak. A gull wooshed out to sea above their heads. Startled to find them there, it shot upwards instead of down, screaming around them. Tom's fingers dug into her arm, steadying her.

'It's all right,' he repeated. 'Only a bird.'

'I know.'

'I'm going to lead you.'

'I can't move, I told you. Not yet.' She was battling to sound calm.

'Your legs will do what you want. You've only got to want, Linda.'

And that was the problem. The want was missing. Terrified of falling off, she could not trust his assurance that it was safe to move. All along he had been saying it was all right and yet it had not been. How dare she trust those words now?

He gave her a slight tug.

She resisted, pulling away. The stone she was holding slid along the surface she was pressing it against.

He had an idea. 'Why don't you drop that stone and take my hand?'

'I can't.'

True, her fingers would not uncoil. How could she shuffle along the ledge, how could he demand it of her, when her hand would not relinquish a useless stone?

He strengthened his hold on her arm and drew her to him. 'Don't look down, just come sideways towards me.'

With eyes shut she made the first minute movement in his direction. Then another.

But she knew that in a moment or two, if she kept this up, she would be in an intolerable situation *because she would have to let go of the tuft of grass*. Deliberately postponing it she kept her next move infinitesimal.

He yanked at her arm, said impatiently: 'Let the grass go. I've got hold of you, you won't fall.'

Under her feet the surface was friable. She heard it crunch as she slid her left foot sideways. And then she reached the dreadful moment, and she came to a halt. To take her right foot up to meet the other one, she must let go of the grass.

For a few seconds she hung there, her right arm outstretched, fingers locked on the grass. He continued to draw her towards him. She let him do it although she kept tight hold of the grass until she faced a clear choice between Tom and it.

Again she stuck. Then, with a rush of courage, she relaxed her grip. Grass dragged through her fingers. After a few more shuffling steps she dropped the pebble. Quite soon the whole thing was over.

They zigzagged across the country, reached the other sea on a blustery day and walked arm in arm along an empty esplanade. A piece of a Victorian pier lingered dangerously. Cafes were shut. In an amusement arcade teenage boys shoved money into slots, their arms mechanical. A poster left over from last summer offered faded coach trips to similar places.

'England!' she said, and laughed.

'Then come to Scotland.'

'No, too far.'

'We could have been there in the time . . .'

'Since I first said that. Yes, I know.'

'Well, then.'

She turned away from him and watched the reckless waves.

Waking early next day she felt his absence and through the hotel's crinkled net curtain saw him scrunching over the beach. It was a beautiful calm morning. Gulls drifted in a pale blue sky. A milk float was creeping along the esplanade. Tom slipped, his feet gouging a mark that stayed dark and wet after he had regained his balance and gone on.

Something tugged at her, threatening her fragile enjoyment of him. She was cross with herself for being unable to clarify, and also because she seemed ready for her fun with him to be spoiled. Although she did not want him to be part of her real life once she went home, she saw no reason to end the holiday adventure just yet.

Over breakfast she reminded him to telephone the garage and check whether his car had been repaired. 'They've had ample time.'

'It all depends when Fanbelts were able to get hold of the part.'

Their proper name was Fanshawe but name-twisting was one of his traits. He was still, when he chose, calling her Maggie, particularly, she noticed, in front of other people so that it was a private joke between them. He had done it at this hotel too.

She said: 'The garage told you three days.'

'Three minimum,' he corrected.

She did not remember it that way but she had not been to the garage with him. Presumably he had been optimistic when he told her three. He left her at the table while he telephoned. As he returned she saw from his face that it was bad news.

'They can't get it yet. Apparently they've had to send to Coventry.'

Linda grimaced. 'We could have driven there and fetched it ourselves if we'd known.' She finished her coffee and pushed back her chair. 'I'm going to buy a postcard.'

'You'll need a coat. It's quite cold out.'

'No, I can get one here. There's a rack of them by the reception desk.'

Some were sepia and some were coloured, all of them were dreary. She became self conscious about the amount of time she was taking over them and felt obliged to buy one. Other guests were having bills made up and checking out, and she was repeatedly in the way. Tom took their bags out to the car. Linda requested the bill but he returned in time to pay it. He had a resistance to her settling bills, although he would accept a cheque from her to cover her share. She had insisted on that.

'I'll drive,' he offered.

'All right, but I want to post this card before we leave here.'

Sitting in the passenger seat she wrote the card, using her shoulder bag as a desk to rest it on.

'It's for Mr Wilkins, the jeweller.'

When she had stuck on the stamp, Tom asked to see the card.

'What a dreary picture.'

Laughing she said that had been her own word but all the cards were equally bad.

He did not hand it back to her but put it on the dashboard on his side of the car. After driving a few hundred yards he pulled up, saying: 'I'll drop it in the box over there for you.'

For a moment she looked at the red pillar box and Tom heading towards it. Then she watched the sea instead. Far out there was the low outline of a tanker. Sea wrack floundered near the shore. On the beach a boy aimed stones and on the esplanade a pensioner in a checked scarf was gazing out to sea, ostensibly unaware that his dog was fouling the pavement.

Tom drove and he drove them to Scotland.

Linda protested: 'Hey, you're hijacking me.' But she was laughing again. They both were.

'We'll come back the minute you can honestly tell me you hate it. OK?'

She leaned back and stretched her legs. Sun was fighting through cloud and scattering thin shafts of gold over the moors. She tried to work the image into her poem, after the sequence about the death of a marriage, but her mind would not grapple with the technicalities of it. She was distracted by beauty and by Tom and by letting him carry her away to the north.

Later that day they hit a sheep. As they dipped into a stretch of dead land, the animal began wandering across. Tom tugged the steering wheel to the right but the road was too narrow. He slammed into the ram's hind quarters.

Linda had been flung forward as he braked, then she was grabbed by her tightening seat belt. Pain seared her left shoulder. With an instinctive gesture, she stuck out her hands to push the creature out of the way.

After the thud of impact there came the rasp of metal tearing on tarmac. Briefly she saw the sheep tumbling along the road and then they overtook it.

'Jesus.' Tom cut the engine and got out.

Linda struggled to look back but her belt was clutching her and it was a few seconds before she could shuck it off. Tom was on the road, blocking her view. She got out, keeping hold of the car door for support. Her legs were wobbly. She could not rid herself of the silly notion that a sheep was made of springy wool and it ought to have bounced without a sound.

Tom was bending over it, then dragging it by the horns until it was at the side. With his foot he pushed it down the tilt and away from the road. A couple of ewes looked up from their foraging but the others took no notice.

'Dead,' said Linda as Tom walked back to the car.

'No.' He went round to the front, where the bumper hung down.

'Well, it must be terribly injured. You gave it a real thump.'

He was sharp. 'I couldn't help that. It got in the way.'

'All right. I only meant it's badly wounded.'

He bent down and tried to straighten the bumper.

She said: 'Tom, what shall we do?'

'Straighten the bumper and go on our way.'

Disbelieving, she laughed. 'No, about the sheep. Are we supposed to report sheep, the way we report dogs we hit?'

'Not unless you want to buy some farmer a sheep.'

'But dogs . . .'

'. . . have licences. That's the difference.'

Linda said: 'All right, forget the farmer. But we can't just leave a badly wounded animal.'

Tom gave her a withering look and went to fetch tools from the car boot. She felt her anger rising and rather than escalate the argument into a row, she walked down the road to where he had dumped the sheep.

The ram lay on its side. It was quivering and seemed unable to move except for rolling wild eyes as she drew near. She could not see any blood, not on the fleece and not on the road. Linda pressed the back of her hand against her mouth, stemming a rush of pity. It was only a sheep, a stupid sheep that had thousands of acres of free range but preferred to potter about on the strip of highway.

She glanced all round, hoping for help of some sort. There was a great emptiness beneath a greater sky, and there was no one there except herself and Tom. Taking a deep breath she returned to the car.

'Tom, we absolutely can't leave that animal as it is.'

On cue, a sheep began to moan. Tom flung down the tool he was using to lever the bumper back into shape. He took a step towards her. She flinched at the tone of his voice.

'OK, Linda, what do you suggest then?'

'I'm going to phone the police and report it.'

'Oh yes? And where are you going to tell them it is?'

'Well . . .'

An unmarked emptiness, a huge sky.

He said: 'There isn't a phone and you don't know where we are. It isn't an option, is it?'

The animal's moans had become a rhythm of distress. Abruptly, Linda ran up the road. She felt useless, committed to helping but incapable. With crazy logic she hoped their sheep was dead, that it was another one crying and that therefore she was not responsible for putting an end to its pain.

But it *was* the sheep they had struck. The sound tore at her. Tom appeared at her elbow.

'Come on,' he said. 'There's nothing we can do.'

'We ought to finish it off.' She hated saying it, her voice was tiny.

'Kill it?'

'Yes, although I don't see how. It's so big.'

She was thinking it would be impossible to smash its head in with a single blow with a stone, or break its neck or do any of the other unpleasant things people were forced to do to deliver the *coup de grâce* to a small dying animal. It was far too big.

Shaming her, he said: 'I don't like shedding blood.'

She flared. 'It's all very well being high-minded but we *ought* to finish it. We injured it and we're the only people here.'

He mocked her with a sly laugh. 'You said yourself you don't know how. Have you got a gun stashed away in the car? Perhaps you carry a humane killer, just in case?'

She was trotting after him down the road. 'This isn't funny. We can't . . .'

'Oh, yes we can.'

Then he had the engine running and the car was inching forward and he was slipping the clutch and playing with her, a threat that he could easily drive off and leave her in all that nowhere, alone. Linda bit back her objections and got in beside him.

He shoved a tape into the machine and the words of her poem filled the car. She hated it. It sounded smug and cosy and artificial. There was nothing of life or death in it. He had killed it.

45

'That metaphor you say is about childhood or old age, the thing about the water . . .'

'Tom, I really don't feel like talking about it.' Or anything else, she meant.

They travelled on in silence. Linda believed they were adjusting their opinions of each other and were neither of them very pleased with what they had learned. No doubt he was accusing her of sentimentality while she was charging him with callousness.

Then her thoughts circled to the dying sheep, and she wondered about the reasons – if sheep could be said to have reasons – that persuaded it to forsake the safety of the land for the road. Did it enjoy the novelty of its hoofs clipping along the smooth surface? Or had it been investigating the nature of tarmac and whether it was edible? To be even more fanciful, could it possibly have known it was doing something dangerous? Victims sometimes courted danger.

She thought about those people who might do it for the frisson, people who indulged in dangerous sports for instance. More mysterious were the battered wives who stayed with violent men. For one reason or for none, people chose to associate with their destroyers.

And then there were the accidents, the blind blunderings towards disaster, and the insignificant choices that led directly to doom. You missed a train and got on the later one that crashed because the driver was drunk. You popped down to the bank on the morning a raider sprayed it with gunfire. You spent years as a hostage because you had delayed filling the petrol tank, not dreaming you would be dashing for the border. You lost your umbrella and accepted a lift in the rain from a friendly motorist at a bus stop who turned out to be . . . Only you never knew what, because you were dead.

She shuddered. Tom flicked a knob and warm air flowed around her feet. She almost said that she was not cold but to point out his misunderstanding meant explaining what made her shudder. As it was a miserable and depressing subject, and they were already in low spirits, she said nothing.

Besides, to explain would be to initiate a discussion of the butcher of Gloucester. That's what they called him in the city, a play on that fairytale tradesman the tailor of Gloucester. Beatrix Potter invented the tailor and gave him a shop by the cathedral, in the alley where Linda lived and reputedly in the same building.

When his business was failing, the author sent an industrious mouse to save him. There was nothing benign in the story of the butcher.

'When I was a kid,' Tom said, breaking into her thoughts, 'I assumed everybody lived by the sea. Don't ask me what I thought all this was about.'

He took a hand from the steering wheel to indicate mountains and unceasing miles of farmland.

Linda said: 'Well, if you were living on the south coast and you didn't have holidays, how would you know?'

'I went to Scotland for the summer, nearly every year.'

'*Did* you?' She was close to challenge. This did not square with the impression she had, of a child idling away summers in a bay where there were pleasure boats, day trippers picnicking with sandy sandwiches on the beach, and a little Hitler of a park keeper who ruined games of hide and seek among the rhododendrons.

Tom was oblivious of her confusion. 'My family had a place up here.'

'Oh?'

'Small, about as hospitable as a shed really. But it was ours, it was a place to go.'

'Do they own it now?'

A shake of the head. 'They sold it. The story was that my father won it in a card game and had to sell it later to pay debts.'

'A pity.' More confusion. She had understood his mother was widowed during his childhood, but this remark suggested not. The coincidence of them both having lost a parent when young had seemed one of the few things they had in common.

He said: 'It wasn't much, it's probably fallen down by now.'

They were approaching a town and Linda was on the alert for bed and breakfast signs. Lights were coming on in the houses.

Tom said: 'I used to think Britain was a long thin strip, with everybody close to the sea. We had it at home and when we got up north, there it was again. It gradually dawned on me that it wasn't like that, but I believed it for years.'

'There's one,' Linda said.

He drove by the sign. 'One what?'

'Place to stay the night.'

But he preferred to drive on. She did not protest. She was not hungry or anxious to stop. After a while she dozed.

*   *   *

47

Linda woke while they were driving through a wood. The road seemed narrow, unfinished. Then she grasped it: they had left the highway, this was an estate road.

'Where are we?' Her voice was sleepy, her tongue furred.

'You're awake? This was to be a surprise.'

'All right, I'm surprised.'

She sat up, stretching insofar as the car and the seatbelt allowed. The road wiggled on, a streak of yellowish dust in the headlights. Pines crowded close.

'Tom, where are we?'

'On the edge of an adventure.'

She could tell from his voice that he was wearing his wicked look. Fumbling in her bag for mints she caught sight of the dashboard clock. It was rather late to be embarking on adventures.

'This adventure,' she began after another quarter of a mile had gone by, 'will it include food and somewhere to sleep?'

At that moment they came out of the trees and there, in a clearing, was a big grey stone house. Tom drew up a short distance from a side door and jumped out. In spite of the hours he had been driving, he was fresh and energetic, hurrying to a window, calling her to join him, then striding about in front of the building. Excited, that was it. He was excited.

Linda gaped. 'It's a *castle*.'

He took the torch from the glovebox and cut the headlights. As he ran past her to the side door, darkness wrapped around her. She was not frightened but she did not fancy being left alone.

'Tom, wait for me.'

A light came on in the building. She found the door wide open on to a stone passage and, stepping inside, called tentatively.

'Tom?'

There were no sounds except the stirring of insects chewing in the beams overhead. The passage was five feet wide and ran for about fifteen feet without doors or windows. Yellowing wire carried power along a wall to a rusty lamp designed to look like a medieval sconce. The electric lightbulb rested wonkily. Calling again, Linda went down the passage. At the end a similar passage joined it on the left but there was no light bulb in this one. She hesitated.

'Tom! Where are you?'

Her voice revealed impatience and frustration. She was not keen to venture beyond the reassuring glow of the wall light but after a moment's doubt decided to try the handle of a door she could see further down.

The room was candlelit. Tom sat at a table made from a slab of oak. A bottle and glasses were reflected in its surface.

'Come on in.' He poured whisky and pushed a glass towards her.

'But . . . Tom, where is everyone?'

'Who?'

'Well, the hotel people . . .' She was standing there, looking around as though they might be concealing themselves in shadowy corners.

He took a slow drink before he replied. 'It isn't a hotel. You said yourself, it's a castle.'

'All right, where are the castle people?'

'We can be the castle people.'

Her bewilderment delighted him. She spluttered questions he did not exactly answer because he was having too much fun teasing her.

Then he said: 'I told you my family owned things in Scotland.'

'Yes, but . . .'

'I know. I didn't admit to a castle.'

She stroked the polished surface of the table. Then she lifted one of the candlesticks, exclaimed at its weight, steadied it with her other hand and began to move about the room. There were dim paintings in glinting frames, and a gaping fireplace bearing the black trace of log fires.

'I've stepped into a dream,' she said, rejoining him at the table.

'Your dream, not mine.'

Some mornings they compared dreams. They did not dream similar things. She had a recurring one about teapots multiplying until she was crowded out of her bedroom. Slightly threatening, she said, although certainly not a nightmare.

But he had said: 'That's a silly dream.'

His own were thrilling ones about chasing or being chased. He denied having any unwelcome ones.

Linda set the candlestick back on the dining table and sat opposite him. Wavering flames made his features indistinct.

Grave as a child she told him: 'I'm in a dream, and I don't want anything to spoil it.'

'I've told you, my dreams are all happy ones.'

He reached across and squeezed her hand, then chided her for not having touched her drink. Obediently she sipped, although she felt empty and did not want it. Tom topped up his own glass. Then he rose. Realising he was going to flick on the torch, she stopped him with a little cry.

'Oh, no! No, you mustn't spoil it.'

Laughing, he slipped the torch in his pocket and took up one of the candlesticks. 'Very well, we'll do the candlelit tour instead. You can carry the bottle.'

He guided her through the castle, admitting: 'I'm skipping rooms, this is highlights only.'

'Mmm, I love the candlelit highlights.'

In reality, it was fairly dull. He showed her a hall which was a high, airy room but not an appealing one; a library with a suspicion of damp about it; a series of sitting rooms dotted with lumpish furniture. If you liked solid Victorian, it was acceptable. Linda always found it dispiriting.

'How old is the building?' she asked. Her view of the exterior had been so limited it was possible the place was Victorian pastiche although she doubted it.

'Hush, you don't ask questions in dreams.'

'Oh, you can, it's just that the answers seldom make sense.'

Candlelight played over portraits along an upstairs passage. They chose a room, the richest, fanciest room with a high bed. Tom set the candlestick on the dressing table and stood her in front of the mirror. Then he gathered her hair in his hands and looped it about her head.

'It would suit you to wear it shorter,' he said.

She felt a pang of disappointment at those words. It was tantamount to him telling her he did not love her any more, which was a foolish way of seeing it because he had never suggested he did love her. He did not use words like love, she had noticed that. She shook her head to free her hair but he held her tight for a moment until his lips brushed her neck in a kiss. Then he released her and she turned to kiss him, her face upturned to his in the candlelight. They climbed into the high bed and made love.

'We forgot supper,' she said afterwards. And so they had.

'We have your peppermints. We won't starve.'

She wanted to wash and clean her teeth but that involved fetching overnight bags from the car, and doing that meant giving up the dream. Instead, she decided to think about something else, and soon she was asleep.

Dawn woke her. They had not closed curtains or blinds and she caught her breath, unprepared for the view of sea and islands glimmering beyond the deep green of the pines. With a glance at Tom's huddled shape, she dragged on her clothes and left the room.

It was disconcerting to be in this large clean empty house and not understand why she was there. Snatches of the previous night's conversation came back to her, but all she remembered was her questioning and his parrying.

Downstairs she found a cloakroom and turned on a tap over the washbasin. Not a drip. Then she spotted a tap on the supply pipe in a corner of the room and twisted that round. After a moment's gasping, brownish water spattered into the washbasin. She turned it off and went outside.

The morning was fresh. A breeze was releasing scent from the pines. She leaned into the unlocked car, reached her travel bag and rummaged in it for her sponge bag. This had a way of working itself to the bottom. While she was smiling at the conceit of the wandering sponge bag, her eye was attracted by a corner of green plastic projecting from beneath the driver's seat. She tweaked it.

Out came a flat package swathed in scuffed green plastic. Inside was a folder, about six inches long by four wide, with stiff and shiny green covers. It was an album, the kind with transparent sleeves to hold photographs. Half a dozen sleeves had been filled with portraits of women, the rest were spare and waiting.

When she had flipped through it, Linda wrapped it up again and was about to replace it under the seat when she thought that as it had fallen out of Tom's bag, she might as well put it back in there for him. His bag was on the rear seat, unzipped and tipped forward. To make space for the album she needed to set the bag upright and press the contents down. She slid a hand into the bag.

Paper scratched her forearm and her exploring fingers drew out a bundle of fifty pound notes. Her curiosity inflamed, she tugged the bag closer, lifted up clothes and discovered a deep layer of bank notes. She had the impression they were also fifties. She buried them again and left the bag looking as though it had not been disturbed. Finally she put the plastic package beneath the seat where she had found it.

Then she ducked out of the car, hoping that if Tom were watching she would appear unconcerned. Her head throbbed with questions she was convinced he would dodge. Why all that cash? Who were the young women in the album? Where were the people who owned the castle or had the right to sleep in it, as she and Tom patently did not?

51

She had stern questions for herself too. *'How on earth did I get into this? And no, I can't blame my resolution to be more trusting. That excuse won't work. I've been fooling myself too long about that. What I'm doing, trailing around with Tom, is plain crazy. So, when am I going to put an end to it?'*

And then a different voice filled her head, her mother's voice, shouting at her: 'Stop dramatising, Linda!' the way it had been shouted during a row about teapots, of all things.

Questions, and accusations, came easily but not the answers. She sensed she had got herself into a situation that was tricky to talk her way out of. For one thing, Tom would not be listening when she tried to talk her way out. If she was sure of anything about him, it was that.

The breeze became a flurry of cold wind and the door banged shut. She shrugged, not caring that she was locked out, and set off along the front of the building, past the crenellated towers. Grey stone in a grey morning, not a pretty sight but she was pleased to note she had been right to reject the idea of Victorian pastiche. Maybe a little nineteenth-century titivating had gone on but the original building was clearly far older.

She attributed the fountain to the Victorians though. Linda squeezed toothpaste on to her brush and cleaned her teeth. There was something deliciously eccentric about doing this in the open air. She was almost laughing except that laughter got in the way of brushing. Foam speckled the surface of the pool, circling for a while before dispersing very slowly. For those few minutes at the fountain she was happy.

Then a small stone hit the ground and bounced close to her. She gave a start, then looked to see what had sent it flying. Nothing, only the wind swaying the treetops. But as she finished brushing, she felt someone's eyes on her and she jerked her head up. Movement gave him away. Tom was on one of the towers, his arm raised.

'Caught in the act,' she thought. *'Another stone.'*

But he turned the movement into a wave. 'Good morning, Linda. Come on up and see the view.'

'It's magnificent from here. This will do for me.'

He argued that up there was better but she was not tempted. The very idea of standing by that parapet made her quake. All at once she felt anxious to get out, get away and lead her own life. She had an urge to drive off and leave him there, just like that. He liked adventures, he often said so, and he admired audacity. Well, wouldn't it be audacious of her to dash off?

While she was thinking this, she was hurrying to the car, keeping close to the building in the hope that he would not hang right over the edge to spy on her.

'*The car key,*' she thought. '*He was driving yesterday so I haven't got it.*' Then: '*Never mind, I'll wire the engine. Won't be the first time.*'

Her steps quickened and she crossed to the car, in full view of him if he were still on the tower.

Another thought came to her. '*Suppose he saw me with the money? I've no idea how long he's been up there.*'

When she had the car bonnet up, and was remembering what to connect, she heard his footsteps. She looked round, her hand sliding to the dipstick instead.

'I'm checking the oil,' she lied.

He stood over her while she did it. 'Does it use much?'

'No, not for a car of its age. This is just one of my better habits. Could you pass me some tissues, please?'

She used a bunch of them to wipe the stick and then tried to clean her hands. His presence had made her nervous and she had touched messier things. Black grease was smeared across her knuckles.

He dropped the bonnet. It seemed like impatience. Then he was swinging her car key. She wished she could take it from him but she needed to clean her hands first.

She said: 'I've got some spirit in my bag, that will do it.'

She worked a splash of it into her skin and the grease disappeared. Tom strode round to the driver's door.

Quickly she said: 'I'll drive, if you like.'

But he was getting into the driving seat, apparently not having heard her. She stuck her head through the open passenger door and told him: 'I'd like to drive.'

'It'll be quicker if I do.' He patted the passenger seat, encouraging her to hop in and let them be on their way.

'What's all the hurry?' she asked, trying to sound normal, not burdened with the knowledge that there were thousands of pounds lying on the back seat, and not guilty to be planning to ditch him.

'Breakfast. Aren't you starving? We didn't even eat your peppermints last night.'

She handed the packet of sweets to him, still not getting into the car. He slid the key into the ignition. She said: 'I need to go back inside.'

For a second she thought he was going to resist, a look of exasperation swept over his face. But he took a key from his pocket and walked her to the side door. As she closed the cloakroom door, he was hanging around in the passage.

The tap was dripping. She ran it hard until the brown water cleared and then she splashed her face and washed her hands. Her mind was on the car key. Surely he had left it in the ignition? If he decided to use the cloakroom when she came out, then she could drive away if she wanted to. She was no longer sure about that.

When she came out, he was in the passage. She felt like a prisoner, escorted to and from the toilets. Tom was talking about what they might do next. Really it was rather like all their other mornings, the only difference was in her head.

Another scheme for escape occurred to her. *'I can dash to the car while he's locking the house. It won't allow me long but it'll be enough.'*

They reached the end of the passage. Linda took a few quick steps as though she was speeding by to avoid impeding the locking up. Once through the door, she broke into a trot.

'Damn. The passenger door's wide open. No time to shut it. I'll race off and see to it when I've gone a few hundred yards. Should be all right unless it clouts a tree.'

She flung herself into the driving seat. The key was in the ignition. Her fingers closed on it.

But Tom stepped in front of the car, saying: 'Hey, I didn't know you were a sprinter.'

'You don't do so badly yourself.' She never knew how she managed to sound so unbothered. Her heart was thudding, she felt foolish and incompetent. Most of all she felt guilty.

Then he was in the passenger seat, adjusting the safety belt. 'It's a beautiful day for a drive up the coast. Why don't we have breakfast in that village, Whatsitsname, about three miles after we rejoin the road?'

'Fine.'

Linda swung the car round. That was something she had not taken into account in her madcap schemes to escape: the car was facing the wrong way. She pictured what would have happened, Tom leaping in front of it and preventing her leaving without him, because she could not deliberately run him down. Then she realised that this was what he had actually done.

They reached Whatsitsname and had breakfast, exactly as he planned. Then they decided what to do for the rest of the day, or rather he made suggestions and she fell in with them. Some of the places he proposed visiting had such fanciful names that she said yes without knowing where they were.

Once she had eaten she felt calmer and as the hours went by so her morning panic came to seem an aberration. She was glad her attempt at flight had failed and wondered how short a distance she would have travelled before coming to her senses and rescuing him.

Tom drove for the rest of the day while Linda watched scenery. She felt lazy. It was luxurious, like having her own personal guide and chauffeur. He regaled her with local history alongside his own recollections.

She appreciated his jokes, did not mind his teasing and was content. But once, when she cast a backward glance, her eye fell on his bag and she was reminded of the bank notes. Misgivings revived until she was sidetracked by the realisation that if she had left him she would have stolen the money. More than that, she might have got clean away with it because how could he call in the police? People did not carry vast sums around unless it was money they had come by illicitly. Loot, then. That's what she had sitting on the back seat of her car. Loot.

5

The woman noticed how the bars of her cell cut the night into vertical slabs of black. The sea, urgent and restless, cried through the dark hours. She could smell mountains on the wet wind. When daylight broke she saw first the jagged whiteness of waves rolling on the shore. Next there was an expanse of uniform greyness that gradually lightened until the scene was divided laterally: the beach outside her window, the sea, the coastline of the main island, and the mountains that sawed the sky.

With the dawn came a cold wind. It excited the waves, swirled dust along the beach and forced her back from her window. She sat on the shelf, in a corner where she was protected from the wind but could not see out. Her hair was like a cosy scarf around her neck but the rest of her body was cold. Movement was painful. She craved a hot shower and a change of clothes almost as much as she craved food and drink. Rubbing stiff limbs, she brooded.

Her mood swung round to anger. She had run out of excuses for him. He had kept her a day and a night alone on an island, without caring what became of her. She rehearsed what she would say when he came. If he were unable to return himself he ought to have sent someone. In his place that is what she would have done; it was intolerable that he should treat her like this; even if he had no idea she was trapped in the cellar, he had abandoned her on the island; no doubt he had found a warm bed for himself. His behaviour was the epitome of selfishness.

A different thought interrupted her flow. No, *no*, she would not think about that, it was too dreadful. He had done reckless things that she knew of and she suspected worse, but it was silly to dwell on them now. She must not dramatise. Yet she could not shake free of the fear.

She ran to the window, shrieking for help, then screaming without words, throwing her voice out over the water. Didn't sound travel long distances over water? Was there not a chance someone stirring in the quiet of early morning would hear her anguish? She shouted until her throat felt raw.

Birds on the strand reacted by taking to the air, circling inquisitively before settling further off. The more nervy ones coasted out to the rocks revealed at low tide. She yelled abuse at them for their indifference to her plight and their ability to go away.

Then she flounced from the window and attacked the door, flinging herself on it, fists and boots hammering. The door was solid, neither rattling nor shuddering under the assault. Next, the ceiling. What she saw was emulsioned plaster, but what was the layer above it? Overhead was the bedroom. She tried to recall what the floor of it looked like.

She remembered plenty of other things about the room. Her wristwatch, for instance, on the table beside the single bed where she lay sleeping while he tiptoed away from the island. Or her bag being lifted up and revealing a folder on the floor beneath it. But what was the floor made of? She was clear that the adjoining kitchen had rough flagstones and so did the bathroom. The difference was that they were built on the ground whereas the bedroom stood over the cellar. Quite possibly the floor was made of boards.

Eager to test this, she cast around for something she could use to gouge. Sticking out of one wall were a few iron nails but tugging confirmed they were unshakeably fixed. The only tool was the flat tin. During the night she had used it to urinate in, carefully emptying it outside her window. Then she had wiped it on one of her tissues, and put that to dry ready to use it for the same purpose if the need arose again.

Standing on the shelf she gained enough height to reach the ceiling and began scraping with a corner of the tin, blowing at the plaster dust as it was released into the air and drifted down on her. After several minutes of this her arm and her neck ached and she needed to get down from the shelf and relieve them. On the ceiling was a shallow groove.

Disappointed, she tossed the tin aside. It was hopeless to think she could break through to the bedroom. How many hours would it take with that tin before she had a hole large enough to squeeze through, always assuming she could hoist herself up to it anyway? Then she examined the rock wall and jumped up on the shelf and ran her fingers over the cold stone. If ever she made a big enough hole, this was her way up to it. There were enough crevices and ledges to make it seem a practical possibility.

She went to the window. The wind had veered enough to allow her to stay there. She took the peppermints from her pocket. Half of them had gone, more than she realised. This frightened her because she could not account for them all and as she needed to eke them out it was important to be disciplined. Putting the packet away she shouted again, thinking that for all she knew there might be boats passing close although not within her view. It was worth the effort of trying to attract them, certainly it was. She shouted, and went on shouting until she recalled what it was like on board a boat. You heard nothing but the sound of the engine.

Unwrapping a peppermint she broke it carefully in half, holding it over her palm to catch the crumbs. Then she licked up the crumbs, let them dissolve on her tongue and swallowed down the slick of sugar before putting one of the pieces into her mouth. The other one went back into the packet.

Hunger had become as much a part of her as hair or toenails. It was a knot in her stomach, an emptiness that, by a curious paradox, seemed to grow and consume her. Her antidote was her anger, at fate and at the man who had taken the boat and gone. When hunger threatened to demoralise her, she became angry about that too, demanding to know how it had happened that we let ourselves be schooled to expect several meals a day, which was neither what our forebears had enjoyed nor what we needed for survival.

What a waste of time it all was, she thought. All that buying and preparing and eating; all that sleeping; all that waiting around. Lives were squandered in repetitive activities so dull that when asked what they had been doing people quite honestly replied 'Nothing much.' Whole lives went by in nothing much. The significant or interesting events in a life could be contained in a space of weeks if not days. She fancied a way of magically editing lives so that people had to live only the worthwhile parts and were spared the bus queues, the extra mealtimes and that third of life that was spent asleep. She had the glimmer of an idea for a poem about it.

The day warmed up. Crows came to peck at the dead sheep. Once she saw a small scuttling creature, maybe a rat, running over it. The sheep had lost more of its sheep shape, it was a sagging mass of wool.

She daydreamed about the man leaving the house, trotting down the beach to the jetty that was a few yards further to her left than she could see. She pictured him skirting the dead animal, perhaps pausing to look at it, then giving a puzzled shrug and hurrying on to the boat. He might well have been puzzled, as she was herself because she had no recollection of the sheep being there before that day. She speculated what had killed it, wondering whether it had toppled from a path above the beach or whether illness had overcome it while it was browsing among the tufty vegetation where the beach met the rising land that was too low to call a cliff and yet marked the great boundary between the shore and the proper land. For a long while she daydreamed like this, her mind skittering from one idea to another.

Sometimes she thought about the man, about his series of women and whether he had brought any of them to this island. She caught herself looking around the room for clues to past presences, then gave a harsh laugh. To imagine such a thing was to give credence to her fear.

Besides, there would be no clues. This was a domestic place, not like the Tower of London where famous prisoners had scratched their initials into the walls. And yet she got to her feet and went looking for marks to interpret as writing. Below the nails were scuff marks made by things that had hung there. That was the best she could do. The rest were smudges and blemishes much less defined.

Engine noise sent her flying to the window. The sea was empty and yet she was convinced she heard an engine, not close but distinct. She crammed herself into the recess, pressing her face towards the bars, trying to make out which direction the boat was travelling. Still no sight of it but it was growing louder. She tussled with the bars as though energy would be sufficient to make them yield. Then she tore off her jacket and her sweater to make herself slimmer, and she ripped off a pink sock, the brightest thing she possessed, and she wriggled into the recess. The sock became a flag waved from a window. But there was no boat.

The engine was dwindling away, exactly as it had done during the night. And then she saw it, a flicker of movement against the flank of a mountain as a little aeroplane puttered down the chain of islands.

Dispirited and tired she put the sock and the other clothes back on and crouched by the window, arguing whether this disappointment merited the comfort of half a peppermint. It did, but what held her back was the depressing knowledge that there might be similar

59

setbacks and she could not afford to compensate every one from her slender supply of food.

So the sweets remained in her pocket and she set her mind to think about pleasanter things, such as the archipelago of which her islet was no more than a dot on the map, and on most maps not even that. She was there by accident, she had never been attracted to such places. Their very isolation deterred her. Why was it that the men in her life were fascinated by them? With her soon-to-be ex-husband she had crossed sandy causeways to rocks where Celtic ruins teetered. Muttering appropriate interest she had kept one eye on the tide. For her the best moment was when he said yes it was time to leave before they were cut off.

Other times they had visited offshore islands on organised boat trips, and she was the only one in the party whose enthusiasm was fake. When people said places were marvellous and full of atmosphere, she concurred. But in her heart she admitted they were forbidding and she was repelled. Although she hoped she sounded agreeable, she could never pretend to enter, as her companions did, into the imagination of a Celtic saint. To be a saint was a rough trade. You lived a lonely life of spiritual torment and you did it on the most inhospitable rock you could find. It was inconceivable to choose such a life.

Stuck in her cell, just beyond the reach of human contact, she felt an empathy with those Celtic hermits.

6

Tom did not mention the money to Linda or accuse her of having uncovered it. He did though make it more obvious that he was paying for everything with cash.

'Perhaps he did so all along and I was unaware,' she thought.

Now that she did know he seemed to be taunting her. When they stopped to fill up with petrol, for instance, he would reach into the bag, withdraw a bundle and peel off a note before tossing the rest back where they had come from. Although she steadfastly gave her attention to something else, the twang of the rubber band was unmistakeable. She was convinced he was doing it deliberately, to draw a comment.

Linda determined not to remark on it, a stance that became increasingly silly as his flaunting of the notes grew more preposterous. Eventually he tipped his bag upside down on one of the twin beds in a hotel room and proceeded to round up and count the bundles. Not noticing was out of the question.

'Looks like you robbed a bank,' she said drily.

'Nothing so brazen. I told you I gave up my business, didn't I? Well, this is the chunk I didn't give up.'

'Ah.' This sounded understanding although she did not really know what he was implying.

He guessed as much and added: 'This is what the taxman didn't see. Some of my clients liked to deal in cash and I can't say I tried to dissuade them.'

She opened her mouth for a repetition of 'Ah' but changed to a question. 'Did you keep it in a bank or under the bed?'

'No point in putting it in the bank, was there? Officially it doesn't exist, so it can't go through the books or into the bank.'

He was smiling a superior little smile at the daftness of her question, he could not help it. Linda bridled. She did not think it was an unreasonable question but before she could defend herself Tom had turned back to his counting.

She saw that her original impression had been accurate: the notes were all fifties. That alone seemed enough to justify her wondering about a bank. Could he really have asked clients to pay him in fifties?

Linda sat on the bed and riffled two of the bundles, like a card player with a couple of decks. She did it clumsily, not fast enough to achieve a blur of colour.

'I can't remember when I've held so much cash,' she said, feigning childish glee. But what she was thinking was that in each bundle the numbers were consecutive.

Shortly after, she ran a bath and lay soaking while Tom went down to the bar. It was all very amusing, she warned herself, but it was definitely time to finish with him and return to her sensible life. No, she would not do anything as peculiar as stranding him, she would be fair and straightforward. Well, as fair and straightforward as she could be without being hurtful. After all, it was hardly his fault that she had been rash enough to become involved with him. On the other hand . . .

A flick of the tap, she topped up the hot water. *'On the other hand,'* she thought, *'it's rather fun and a back seat full of stolen banknotes doesn't make me Bonnie Parker. Tom already has the cash and he's going to spend it, whether I'm around or not. I don't see how I have any responsibility. Not for any of it, actually.'*

Flapping her hands she fluffed up the dying bubbles of bath foam. The truth was she enjoyed his stories even if she did not entirely accept them. Early on she had realised they were not each and every one to be trusted. Either he was an incompetent liar or he was testing her tolerance to inconsistency, but she had not settled which. There was, for example, the widowed schoolteacher mother who had coached pupils in the holidays, resulting in the young Tom being alone on a southern beach all his summers. But there was also the mother whose long holidays from school allowed her to take him to Scotland for weeks on end. Every day she encountered that kind of inconsistency, the kind that was dismissed, whenever she queried, as misunderstanding on her part or simplification on his. A childhood was a long time, he had pointed out, for some of it one thing had been true and for the rest of it another. But it was useless trying to resolve which parts of his tales were reliable and she resolved to give up. None of it mattered, anyway. In a few days

62

she was going home and that would be the end of him. She was almost certain of that.

White foam was subsiding to greyish froth. She reached for a towel, but as she set a foot on the tiled floor she skidded and had to grab the washbasin to steady herself. Her foot left a wet streak on the tiles.

Immediately she looked down at it she remembered something. At last she knew what had troubled her about their second meeting. No skid marks. He had claimed his car had skidded across the lane but there were no marks. And another thing, since then he had not once displayed such incompetence at manoeuvring a vehicle.

In the mirror she saw her rueful expression. '*A ploy to get to know you,*' she told her mirror image.

Then she turned away from the reflection of her own eyes accusing her of being a dupe, and she rapidly dried and dressed. By the time she had chosen which earrings to wear, she had reverted to thinking that even if it was entertaining to be an innocent kind of Bonnie Parker, what she was actually going to do was call a halt to it. Tomorrow. No point in spoiling tonight, she would do it tomorrow. Definitely.

Through the wall a television blared and before the volume was turned down a voice began reading news headlines. Linda switched on her set but was disappointed to learn it was only a regional news bulletin. There had been a road smash, a house fire, a factory closure, and a development in the story about a baby who had undergone two organ transplant operations. Fascinating if you were local, it was strictly not for tourists. Linda switched off the set, put on her earrings and went down to join Tom.

Telling him next morning was difficult. He seemed happy, rushing around with such an air of excitement that she could not steel herself to spoil it.

As she came out of the bathroom, rubbing her wet hair with a towel, he turned off the television and pitched into a discussion of their route that day. They had been over it the evening before, Linda feeling guilty about her insincerity but sticking to her plan not to ruin their final evening. And now he was making it hard for her, simply because he was happy.

He jabbed a finger on the map he had spread out on the bed. 'We get the boat here. See?'

'I didn't realise we had to get on a boat.'

63

'Of course we get on a boat. A ferry. We're going to an island.'
'I know it's an island but I thought there was a bridge.' She flung the towel down on a chair and shook out her hair.
'A bridge?'
'Or one of those . . . What's the other thing they have?'
'A causeway? Well, our island has a ferry. It's a proper island.'
Teasing her, he lunged and caught a handful of her hair, holding it up and making scissoring motions with his free hand. 'Come on, Linda, when are you going to get it chopped? You'd look great with one of those really short crops.'
She squirmed free, squealing that she liked it the way it was and he was to leave it alone.
He was mildly derisive. 'Not very adventurous, are you?'
'I didn't claim to be.'
Neither had she told him about her stock-taking session and her resolutions. She was glad of that because he would have been merciless. All he knew was that she was divorcing and taking up a new life that included poetry.
Later she wished she had spoken up right then and refused to go to the island, regardless of whether it had a bridge, a causeway or a ferry. But instead of saying outright that she wanted to go home, she sought a gentler, circuitous way out.
'We'll check on his car first,' she thought. *'If it's ready I'll make it the reason to end all this.'*
Aloud she said: 'How long is the crossing?'
They talked about boats and tides until it was time to go down to breakfast. Over the sausages, she reminded him to telephone the garage.
He said: 'That can wait until tomorrow.'
'If it were my car I'd want to know exactly what's going on.'
He started brushing the matter aside again but she persisted until he gave way and agreed to telephone before they left the hotel. While she was drinking a second cup of tea he went up to their room to make the call.
A man who had finished reading his newspaper offered it to her as he left the dining room. It was a Scottish paper, not one she would have chosen. There was a picture of a road smash, a sad photograph of a toddler with two transplanted organs, and there, on the second page, was a story about a fire. Linda gasped.
Afraid she was drawing attention she glanced around, but the other guests were preoccupied with their food, their companions,

or their own newspapers. She checked whether Tom was coming back and for the first time in her life caught the eye of a waitress who sped to her table and asked what else she would like to order. Flustered, Linda asked for more tea.

With the waitress on her way to the kitchen, she tried again to read the report of the fire but could not hold the paper steady. Pushing crockery aside she laid it down. Type stopped shimmering and the photograph became clear. Dorris Castle, she read, was severely damaged. The blaze in the fifteenth-century building had been discovered the previous afternoon when forest workers spotted smoke. The castle, which had been extensively renovated by a favourite of Queen Victoria, was owned by a peer who lived in Paris. It had been on the market for two years. And so on.

Dorris Castle was where she and Tom had spent a night. The following afternoon it was in flames. Linda felt sick, and then ashamed that it took several minutes before she was willing to concede he might have had nothing to do with it.

The fresh tea came and she drank it scalding hot, automatically, not wanting it at all, her hand going for the cup and her mouth swallowing without her taking any interest in the actions. Her mind was elsewhere, baffled and suspicious, guilty and alarmed.

'*He hated me going back inside,*' she remembered. '*He was in a rush to drive away. He accompanied me right up to the cloakroom and out again. He hated me being there.*'

But she could not recall any details that made him appear culpable of setting the fire. He had been anxious to leave? Well, he was famished. He had stuck with her as she went in and out? Well, he was making sure she did not linger because he wanted to get to Whatsitsname and eat.

No, there was nothing odd about his behaviour at the castle, except for the extremely odd matter of taking her there at all. She wondered whether . . .

A hand stroked her hair. She leaped, slopping tea.

'Hey, you're jumpy.' He dropped into the seat opposite her.

Dabbing with her napkin at splashes on her blouse she mumbled about having been miles away and not hearing him coming. He leaned across and took the newspaper. It was open at the report of the fire. What would he say? Linda waited for him to speak, studying him from the corner of her eye. He was reading, then he was folding the paper.

'No joy with the car,' he said. 'Someone at Coventry screwed up Fanbelts' order.'

She dragged her attention back to the garage, the car and the phone calls to speed things up. 'Does this mean the garage doesn't have the part yet?'

'That's right. They're still waiting.'

'But that's ridiculous.'

He shrugged. 'That's what I told them, only rather more energetically. They say they'll send someone over to collect it.'

'Really?' This was such an abrupt change of attitude that she could not help sounding dubious.

Tom qualified it. 'Not a special trip, I didn't mean that. Apparently one of the mechanics is going over that way in any case so he'll pick it up.'

'When?'

'Tomorrow.'

Tomorrow, and presumably the garage would set to work on the engine the following day and perhaps it would be a two day job. Linda totted up four more days before Tom and his car could be reunited. She felt muddled, unable to settle on questions let alone answers.

All the imagined farewell scenes faded. Her planned speech was unspeakable, and the latest news about his car guaranteed that she would seem mean if she left him now. She realised how very much she had been relying on good news from Fanbelts to soften his disappointment.

A fresh idea sent her on a new tack. If there was no good news from the garage, then she must provide another compelling reason for them to return south. She needed a few minutes alone.

Linda poured him tea, without asking whether he wanted it. When he began to drink, she said she was going out to a newsagent's shop a few doors away to buy another postcard.

'I hope you find something less dreary than your last effort,' he remarked, turning over the paper to read the sports page.

Linda hesitated in the entrance hall long enough to make sure he was not watching her through the dining room's glass doors. Then she darted upstairs to their room and locked herself in. She looked up a telephone number in her diary, her friend Kathy's number in Yorkshire, and lifted the receiver.

There was a peculiar noise on the line, she could not get through. After trying a few times she called reception and explained.

The redhead behind the desk told her: 'I'm sorry, it isn't connected.'

'I don't understand.'

'It's been disconnected, because the people who stayed there before you left very early. When someone's paying the bill the night before, we fix the phone so they can't make any more calls. I'm afraid we forgot to reconnect it for you.'

'Then how can I make a call?'

'Only from here. Your phone won't be usable until we take it apart and fix it. We've got a problem with our computer and until it's repaired we can only do it manually.'

Linda started to say that Tom had used it a few minutes ago but broke off. Clearly it was impossible. She said she would come down, and asked for the bill to be prepared.

Tom met her as she reached the foot of the stairs. The lies came easily to her: she had left her money upstairs, she had walked as far as the shop and had to turn back.

'I've asked them to do the bill,' she added, to change the subject.

'Good. I'll pay while you go back to the shop then.'

Linda bought two postcards, another one for Mr Wilkins the jeweller and one as a souvenir. When she returned to the hotel, Tom was loading her car, evidence of the way she had let herself be hooked into his plans again. She did not know whether to blame her laziness or her amenable temperament. It was often hard to separate the two.

'You're a fool, Linda,' she thought. *'You're letting him run things and all* you *want to do is run away with him. Why didn't you say you had an invitation from Kathy. You could still do it, it's not too late.'*

But it was. Because she had told the lie about the wasted walk to the newsagent's shop, she had missed the best opportunity to tell the one about a phone call to Kathy and an invitation to visit her in Yorkshire. Every extra minute that passed without it being mentioned reduced the plausibility of the Kathy story.

On the television screen a journalist was talking in front of a building of blackened stone. Then there were aerial shots of smoke clouding a pine forest, and next some footage of firefighters tackling the blaze. Linda recognised the site of the fire as the tower nearest the fountain.

'He didn't mention it,' she thought. *'It was there in the newspaper and he didn't say a word.'*

Behind her the door moved. She spun round.

Tom said: 'I came to fetch the guidebook.'

She had told him she was going up to their room to write. They had argued on the ferry coming over and had been rather quiet since. 'I think we left it in the car.'

She gathered her courage. It was nonsensical to go on pretending. If he had not known earlier that she was aware of the fire, he knew now.

'We were there, at the castle that burned.' She was stating a plain fact, no tinge of suspicion in her voice.

'I know. I didn't want to worry you. I thought you'd be upset.'

'Upset?'

'Thinking that if it had happened sooner we'd have burned in our bed.'

'When did you learn about the fire?'

'It was on television this morning, while you were in the bathroom.'

Linda remembered him switching the set off as she came out, and his eagerness to engage her attention with the map spread on the bed. She said: 'I found out when I looked at the paper.'

'You didn't say anything.'

'Neither did you, Tom.'

He looked closely at her. She anticipated the question 'Why not?' but he did not ask her. There was an uncomfortable pause. She became aware of the television burbling beside her and she pressed the button to kill it.

'Tom, why were we at that place?'

'The castle? Because I wanted to. An adventure, I told you.'

'You didn't have any right to be in there, did you?'

'I had a key, you saw that.'

'You shouldn't have taken me there.'

'I used to go there, I kept the key. That's all.'

She was frowning, dissatisfied that they were circling an issue. Her questions were about moral rights, his answers were about practicalities. This had always been one of the gulfs between them, and it was also among the things she found stimulating about his company, one of the reasons she was unsettled by his conversational manoeuvres.

Linda shifted on to his ground. 'Why did you go there before?'

'I told you my . . .'

'No, they didn't.'

He capitulated with a mischievous laugh. 'OK, it was a joke when I said my family owned it. I worked there once, with a builder the estate office called in to patch up some storm damage.'

'And he had to have a key.'

'Which got mislaid.'

'How long ago was this?'

'Linda, please.'

He always hated her going into what he called her inquisitorial mode, and he had learned how to warn her off. Instead, she went back to the fire. What did he think started it? Could they have had an accident with those candles?

He pooh-poohed the candles and offered no theories of his own. The subject seemed at an end but it was Tom who fanned it back to life a few minutes later.

'There's no need to tell anyone we were there, is there? I mean, it wouldn't do any good because we don't know what happened.'

Once he had her agreement, he went out to the car to seek the guidebook. He said he was going to sit in the bar and browse. She cleared a space on the dressing table and took out her notebook, thinking that whenever he came back she would prefer to be discovered writing than worrying over the castle fire.

Skimming the lines of her new poem, she found herself ambivalent about the second line. A phrase that had seemed apt no longer worked. Too pat, she decided, too comfortable somehow. She jotted a few alternatives at the foot of the page.

When she had written the lines she had been certain of herself, dedicated to particular truths. Now her perception had changed. Tom was influencing her, although he did not know it. When he teased her, when he showed her the money concealed from the Inland Revenue, when he took her to bed in a castle where he had no right to be, on all those and a dozen other occasions he was saying: 'Hey, look, there's another way of living, one you've been too narrow to explore.'

He did not like her poetry, not the taped poem he had heard and not in principle. But his gibes did not belittle her, they encouraged her to be tougher about making time to write. She wondered whether it was really the poetry he disliked or the amount of time she insisted on giving to it, which meant time when she excluded him.

His objections, predictable by now, were about the ambiguities and obliqueness. He liked things clear, he said, because how else was he to be sure he understood? Linda had ended one wrangle by asking, with a measure of sarcasm: 'What was that line of Housman's, about perfect understanding sometimes extinguishing pleasure?'

But it was not an answer to Tom's objections, it was only a sharp way of ending a discussion she found tedious. There was no answer.

A line came to her. She began to write, then hesitated seeking an appropriate word. Her search took her through plunderer, thief and raptor. None of them fitted. She lay down her pen and looked across at Tom's bag sagging on a bench. Softly, nervous of being heard, she slid the bolt on the door. The money fascinated her, she wanted to see it again and feel the weight of those thousands of pounds. Consecutive numbers suggested bank money, not gathered together cash payments from customers. Linda put her hand into the bag and met the layer of bank notes. She felt the anticipated ripple of excitement. Then her flying fingers were investigating a side pocket. The photograph album was in there. She set it down beside the bag and then lifted out the folder where he kept receipts.

The pieces of paper were all there, chronologically. No phone calls appeared on any of the hotel bills. She began looking for excuses. All right, last night's hotel staff had failed to reconnect their phone after protecting themselves against misuse by the previous guests. It was possible Tom could have made his call to the garage from the reception desk instead, and it would not have shown up on the bill unless the receptionist remembered to charge him. But it was improbable there had been a rigmarole about phones at their other overnight stops. Calls could sometimes be overlooked, but not every time.

Every time? Twice, that's all it was, only twice. Two oversights did not amount to much. She winced at her willingness to be suspicious.

'*What are you trying to prove?*' she asked herself. '*That he's a bank robber who's deceiving you about the time his car repairs are taking? Just because he used a trick to get to know you doesn't mean he's guilty of anything else.*'

Guilty or innocent? She so often judged him that way.

Linda took up the photograph album. Seven women. She had thought there were six but in fact there were seven. None of the pictures were formal portraits, they had all been taken outdoors while the woman was laughing or smiling at whoever held the camera. Tom, presumably. One other thing they had in common: there were no other people in the shots, no small figures or traffic in the background. They had been with him in a quiet place and he had photographed them looking happy.

But who were they? Friends or lovers? Their ages appeared to range from the mid twenties to about her age. If they had been lovers, why had love foundered, seven times? Had they intended to be as transient in his life as she did, or had the break-ups been a destruction of hopes?

'Perhaps I'm number eight,' she thought, flippantly counting off the smiling faces until she reached the first empty envelope.

But it was not comical after all. It embarrassed her to classify herself with these anonymous women and think of herself as no better than his latest pick-up. She caught herself wondering whether he had also met them in hotels, staged accidents in lanes, faked reasons for gratitude and dinner, and for moving smoothly into their lives.

Well, so what? That was the way of it unless one resorted to contact groups and lonely hearts columns. Tom's fault lay in being elaborate, or at any rate in being caught out being elaborate.

Linda shrugged off her criticism, knowing it was characteristic of him to complicate matters with mysteries and manoeuvres. It was the way he played the game of life: things are fairly dull and ordinary, so liven them up. Even so, she felt he had stalked her.

She smoothed the empty envelope between her fingers and murmured: 'Number eight?'

Turning the pages she went backwards through the album. Seven was a brunette with long hair and a green shirt. Six and Five were similar types, slightly plump with bobbed hair and T shirts. Four was a delicate blonde with an elfin face and a denim jacket. Number three looked younger than the others. Her mid brown hair was looped up in an untidy knot and she wore dark leggings beneath a long cardigan. Number two favoured big hair and big shoulder pads. Number one was fair with curls, probably a perm.

Why did he keep this album, and carry it around? Not to remind himself of old loves so much as old conquests, she thought.

'Predator,' Linda said to the empty room.

'Was it this island you came to when you were a child?'

They were standing near the harbour watching a fishing boat lurching its way towards land.

71

'No, it was tiny, over to the west.'

'Have you been back?'

'I tried once but the ferries weren't running. I'd left it too late in the year and the weather was bad.'

'Is it as rough as that?'

'Some of the year. If I'd gone in summer it would have been all right but I left it until autumn and the first of the storms was blowing.'

'Haven't you attempted it since?'

He shook his head, looking west, gazing down the years towards his childhood summers.

He said: 'I ought to say something hackneyed about one not being able to go back anyway, how it's always a disappointment. But the truth is I wanted to, very much.'

Such sadness in his voice, it caught at Linda's heart, like all those other stories of his that were really only half-stories because the happy pleasurable things had not quite happened. She squeezed his hand.

'Never too late,' she said.

Tom was silent, very still.

The crew of the fishing boat were clearly visible now, not their faces but their bright plastic garments dipping and diving in a grey scene. Linda's stomach tightened in empathy. She was not a good sailor.

Tom's hand in hers felt warm but leaden. He was like a statue, facing out to sea but with a glazed look that showed he was not seeing anything.

'*Memories*,' she thought. '*A boy playing again on a tiny Scottish island, bringing in peat for the fire in a house that's no better than a shed.*'

You remembered the things you had loved or hated, and the inbetween days blended into a general impression of middling comfortableness, if you were lucky, or discontent if not. Tom remembered the house that was almost a shed, and therefore it was not significant whether he had spent all his holidays there or only a few. It mattered, and that is what mattered.

Linda had a vivid picture in her head of that house. Slate roof and white walls, a low building facing a strip of water between islands; peat cutting scarring the hill above it; a boat, with an outboard motor, rocking beside a stone jetty.

Her confidence amused her. Was she relying on Tom's descrip-

72

tions or scenes on television? Both, probably. Imagination was complicity. A poet says 'This is the way it feels,' and the reader believes because it is the way something different has felt for her. A director aims a camera and says 'This is what a place looks like,' and the viewer trusts the rest to be a continuation of that one carefully composed shot. Someone who is not an artist with paint or camera or words describes a house in plain language, and the listener colours it up.

'I wish I could see it,' she said.

Momentarily, the pressure of Tom's hand increased on hers. Then he exhaled.

'What's to stop you?' His tone made it a dare.

'Well . . . nothing.'

'We'll do it, then.'

Now he was grinning at her, ruffling her hair, making her feel like a nervous child who had to be coaxed into every unknown.

Linda pulled away from him, smoothing her hair and laughing. She was confused. All she had meant was that she wished she could see it, not that she had any intention of jumping on more boats and making the wish come true. Yet it seemed she had agreed to it.

Tom did not allow any backtracking. When she started to say that perhaps it was not such a great idea because it was a long way, he was scarcely listening. The fishing boat was getting close and he was more interested in discussing what the crew were up to, where they had been and for how long, and whether it was worth their while to go out now that the huge factory ships hoovered up the fish before they ever reached the islands.

Before she could impress on him that her second thoughts were serious objections, they were down at the port inquiring about ferries to Tarbert. Linda was wryly amused at the way his enthusiasm was blotting out anything she said. Once, she thought the solution was to delay until the next day, because that would give her time to be sure what she wanted to do. Tom looked mystified, asking what was the point of wasting time when the weather was good? She had to concede that, although the pitching of the fishing boat made the sea look choppy by her standards, for the west of Scotland early in the year it was fair and fine. It was that which swayed her. Why make a rough crossing another day when she could do it in comparative comfort there and then?

It was a wrench to leave her car behind, but he had decided it was for the best. Misgivings showed on her face.

Tom said: 'I know a good place where we can leave it. It'll be quite safe.'

But it was not the business of protecting it from thieves or accidents that bothered her, it was the very fact of parting with it. For days it had been her home. She shared it with him, some days willingly and others less happily, but it was hers all the same. It cocooned her, identified her, gave her shelter and mobility. It had become a piece of her.

She was not the type to be sentimental about objects. She had never been soppy enough to give her cars names, not even her first runabout which her mother had dubbed Calamity Jane because it was always breaking down. Her car was only ever her car, not her brand name Ford, or her model Mini. Her car. It was a mere machine for getting around, a tool for doing the job of travelling. Yet it was difficult to step on to a ferry and leave it behind.

She was slow in getting her bag out of it. Tom chivvied, nervous about missing the boat. Linda said there was lots of time and continued to be slow. She was having to choose what to take and what to leave, without having much idea what she would need at the other end of the trip.

'Tom, you're not being much help.' She appealed to him, garments over one arm and unsure whether they were to go in the bag that was staying or the one that was going with her.

'Take the warm clothes, nothing fancy.'

'But I haven't brought anything fancy.'

'I meant the skirts.'

She tried again. 'Well, how long will we be there? Do I want three days worth of underwear or two? Come on, give me a clue.'

'Um, three. Yes, take three.'

He began sweeping the contents of the dashboard shelf into a plastic carrier bag. Linda asked him why on earth he was doing that.

'Because I'm going to lock everything in the boot.'

'I thought you knew a safe place.'

'Doubly safe if everything's in the boot. OK?'

She said she supposed so, and crammed spare shoes into the bag she planned to take. Tom was feeling beneath the front seats for road maps, an entry ticket to a house they had visited, the wrapper from her peppermints, a handful of things that had escaped attention when she last tidied. She usually kept the car tidy and had never understood why some people treated theirs like peripatetic dustbins.

Tom put the stuff in the boot and locked it. Then he drove her to the ferry terminal and asked her to mind the bags while he took the car to its safe place.

'A lock up garage,' he told her.

The row of garages near the playing fields in Gloucester flashed across her mind. It was less than two weeks but it felt a very long time since she had walked through the damp and the dusk to collect the car and set out on her peculiar holiday. Perceptions of time changed when you broke a routine.

Tom was saying: 'I asked around and an old boy who lives in that bungalow said he doesn't use his garage and I could put it there. He thinks it's his lucky day. He only went into the shop for a packet of frozen peas and by the time he came out he'd rented his garage to a tourist.'

Although he pointed, it was a vague gesture that did not explain to her which one of the scattered buildings was the old man's bungalow. Then he was in the car and moving away.

Linda sat down by the bags. Her spirits slumped. She felt hollow, as though inside her was a black nothingness that was growing and would go on growing until it had consumed her. She wished there was a way to magic herself home, or that she had insisted on a retreat to the mainland, or that the ferry would break down and be unable to go. A shiver ran through her.

There was a telephone nearby. She asked for the number of Fanshawe's garage and spoke to a mechanic who said they did not have Tom's car in for repair. She insisted, foolishly: 'It's a red one.'

'Sorry, miss, whatever colour it is, you've got the wrong garage.'

'Do you have another branch?'

'No, there's only this one. Look, why don't you ring Taylor's?'

She let him give her the number of Taylor's but she had no intention of ringing it. Taylor's was in a different town, one she and Tom had bypassed, and anyway Tom would not have dubbed it Fanbelts.

She hung up and walked around but her legs wanted to hurry her away. A voice in her head was encouraging escape: *'You don't have to go, you're supposed to be a free agent, why don't you get away now while he's not here to persuade you?'*

The word persuade jarred. Tom did not persuade. He made suggestions and followed them through whether she was wholehearted or not. Clear enough when she looked back, it was not always apparent at the time it was happening, and on the occasions it had been, she had failed to deter him. She was unequal to it. She felt stupid to let herself be treated this way, stupid and slightly afraid.

Returning to the bags she hovered over them, poised to snatch hers up and flee. She imagined herself running in the direction he had pointed, meeting him on the road and getting her car key and directions to the garage, making her farewell speech and rushing away before he had recovered from his astonishment. He would have to believe she meant it this time, he would have to accept their adventure was over, and he would have to let her go.

'Are you OK?'

The voice came from her left. Linda saw a young man in an anorak, yellow hair blowing across a weather beaten face.

'Yes, I'm fine.'

'Only you looked so . . .'

'I was daydreaming.'

'That's all right then.' He wore the embarrassed smile people do when they get it wrong.

She expected him to go back to his friends, a knot of men standing around a heap of backpacks and bundles of gear, but he lingered, saying: 'A good day for the crossing.'

'Mmm.'

'Have you done it before?'

'No.'

'The Minch can be a rough passage but not today. Lucky for your first time.'

He had been kind to her and he deserved more than monosyllables. She asked whether he was going walking.

'Climbing. We went to Harris last year, had a fantastic time. Couldn't wait to come again.'

All those drops, all those long empty views. Linda shuddered.

He said: 'Some of the guys wanted to stay and climb here but we talked them out of it. Next year, we said.'

He looked beyond her to the fretted mountains. 'Who was it said they reminded him of Wagner's *Ride of the Walkyries* frozen in stone?'

Then he saw her face and laughed. 'Not your idea of a good time, I see.'

She was laughing too. 'No head for heights. And I had a bad time on a coastal path not so very long ago.'

'Me, it's Underground trains,' he said. 'Absolute panic the day I went up to London and the train stopped in the tunnel between stations. The engine shut down, everything. Panic, only of course you don't show it, do you?'

'Unless you're petrified on a cliff edge. Then you do.'

He pulled a face, conceding her point. 'I do see there's a difference. Physical danger on the cliff, not much on the Underground. Of course, you don't reason at the time, do you? Too busy panicking.'

One of his friends drifted over, pretending he had come to protect her. 'Is he upsetting you, miss?'

'Terribly,' Linda said, 'he's reminding me how I nearly fell off a cliff.'

'Shame, Gerry,' said the friend.

Then one of the others called to them with a problem about some of their gear. The yellow haired Gerry and his friend wandered off.

Inconsequential as it was, the encounter was enough to change her mood. Even though Gerry had unwittingly revived her terrors on the cliff edge, he had raised her spirits. She lifted her bag. She was up to it now. She could brace herself to turn her back on the ferry, locate her car and take charge of her life.

Linda paused, looking at Tom's bag. In it was the money, the album of smiling women, the sheaf of receipts that mentioned no telephone calls, and all the mystery that was Tom's life. Well, goodbye to it. It had been intriguing and enjoyable and a bit scary, and now the adventure was over.

And yet she hesitated to walk away and leave the bag all on its own, a miserable illustration of the cruel way she had ditched him. He would come back and find it standing there, with the climbing party and a handful of other passengers a few yards away, and everyone knowing the significance of Tom's lonely bag. She jibbed at humiliating him publicly.

So she considered leaving the bag in the safe-keeping of Gerry and his friends. They seemed decent people, although how on earth did one tell? Unless they troubled to open it, they would have no idea it was stuffed with banknotes. Of course, as they did *not* know, the chance of them opening it was greatly reduced.

Tempted, she was already choosing the words for asking Gerry to take the bag, when it occurred to her that in a way it was worse to do that than leave the bag on its own. A lonely bag would arouse speculation, but to hand it over to Gerry would put her treachery beyond doubt.

She started to walk away. People were watching her, she sensed them, but there was nothing in the manner of her going that suggested drama. In her head she was rehearsing the brief conversation she would have with Tom when they met, and she came to realise that abandoning his bag had been shrewd. He would be so anxious to reclaim it that he would not waste time arguing with her. Her bag was heavy and dragging on her arm. She hoisted it to her hip, locked her other arm round it to share the weight and went on. The road took her through a cluster of buildings, and she kept alert for a side street leading off in the direction Tom had pointed.

A shout. She looked over her shoulder and saw him standing in the road behind her. He did not move, he was expecting her to hurry back to him. Linda stayed where she was. They faced each other. Then a car came along and she had to step out of its way, and once she had started moving it seemed absurd not to go on doing so. And so it was Linda who walked up to Tom and not the other way around.

Linda sat in the hired car in Tarbert and listened to the radio. Radio was nearly all that was left of her usual life. Now the car she travelled in had changed. She had lost her name days ago because Tom kept using Maggie. On the boat coming over, when Gerry and his climbing friends had spoken to them, Tom had called her that. Added together, all the little changes, the little losses, gave her a feeling of having become disconnected.

Sometimes, when radio reception was good, she heard programmes from London, but much of the time the voices she picked up were Scottish and unfamiliar. They had a knack of using dialect words or phrases that made them hard to follow.

She moved the knob until she heard people she recognised. Just her luck, she thought, to get a programme she loathed. She twiddled away from it. A Scottish accent was part way through a news bulletin about mishaps in places she had not heard of or, if she had, could not locate on the inadequate map in her mind. Her hand went for the knob again but as the next station she tuned to was broadcasting in Gaelic, she returned to the newsreader. Joining the woman in mid-sentence she heard: '. . . was found beneath rubble in Dorris Castle which was damaged by fire on Tuesday. The identity of the victim has not been established. Inquiries into the cause of the fire are continuing.' A pause. Then: 'In Inverness, fishermen protesting about a three million pound development scheme interrupted a meeting of the . . .'

78

Horrified, Linda switched the radio off and sat, tense, a hand pressed to her mouth.

'A body in the castle,' she thought. 'But wait. Is that actually what I heard? Did she say body? No, no she said something else. Something near to it. Victim. That's it, victim. She said: the identity of the victim. Well, a victim is a body. In this case it must be. Fire, rubble, unidentified victim. It must be a body.'

Hoping the item would be mentioned briefly in a round-up at the end of the bulletin, she switched on again. But she was too late. A man was forecasting the weather.

Linda got out of the car and sought Tom. Once he had hired the car he had driven a short distance and then parked, telling her he was going to make a telephone call to arrange a hotel room for the night. She had assumed they were close to a call box and was surprised when he had walked back the way they had come. She took a few steps in that direction.

The wind was keen. Although the crossing had been calm, or so everyone else on the boat had maintained, the sun had faded. From the sea the mountains of North Harris had been tremendous dark presences flecked with cloud. Snow glared from the peaks. The climbing party had behaved like exuberant children. Excitement was infectious. Tom caught it first and Linda soon succumbed.

She stood, lacerated by the wind, her hair flying. Then she got back into the car thinking that even if she met Tom in the street, she would not want to discuss the fire until they were in the privacy of the car.

'A newspaper,' she thought. 'I'll ask him where we can buy a paper before we leave the town.'

Tom came, burdened with a carrier bag that clinked as he lowered it into the boot. 'For picnics,' he explained.

'Picnics? At this time of year?'

She could not tell whether he was serious. He did not answer but she did not press him because she was eager to talk about the fire. Quickly she checked that he had made a hotel booking, and then she reported what she had heard on the news.

Tom said: 'Just as well we didn't admit to being there.'

His low key response amazed her. She needed to see her own revulsion echoed and he was not doing it. Emphasising her words, she repeated: 'Tom, a body was found in the castle we stayed in.'

'Perhaps someone started the blaze and didn't get out in time.'

'It was found beneath rubble in the burned part.'

'Do they know who she was?'

'She?'

'I thought you said . . .'

'No. All I heard was victim. She said . . .'

'Oh, that's it. The newsreader was she. You confused me.'

Linda snorted. 'I'm pretty confused myself. We break into a castle for the night, after which it goes up in flames and kills someone. Don't you see, we could have been killed ourselves?'

'We didn't break in.'

Brushing aside legal niceties about forcing entry or using a key without permission, she said: 'Whoever this victim turns out to be . . . I'm going to say he, I don't think women have as much taste for arson . . . Whoever he turns out to be, he was probably wandering around in there at the same time we were. What if . . .'

'Hold on a minute. Why don't you tell me exactly what they said on the news?'

'I did tell you but you don't seem to grasp what danger we were in. You don't seem to see how awful it all is.'

When he gave a dismissive shrug, her temper flared. He might have been her mother screaming at her for getting things out of proportion.

'Tom, someone's dead. Do you really think that after this we can creep away without telling anyone we were there?'

'There's nothing we can do about it.'

As he spoke he was starting the engine and pulling away down the road. For a while she battled to make him understand, if not share, her reactions. He did not argue against her, but he sidestepped with remarks such as: 'There's nothing we can do about it.' He said it in a flat voice that discouraged further discussion. After a mile or two she fell silent. It was no good, he did not feel things the way she did.

All the while they were driving on through the desolate countryside.

The hotel was modest and old fashioned, and they were the only guests. Linda puzzled why he had chosen it. They had seen others that looked more inviting than this pebble-harled hulk and which might not have fed them from tins and freezer packs, as this one did.

Perhaps he used to stay there on childhood jaunts, she thought. She decided not to question in case it sounded critical. Memories were fragile, an unkind word could spoil them. But the visitors' lounge was a drab place and she could not endure an evening there. The only item of interest was a map, pinned to the wall, that showed the chain of islands. At a glance they looked like the floating skeleton of a dinosaur. Tom was studying the map, so Linda said she was going upstairs to write.

It was an excuse to get away, she had nothing to write. Her thoughts were still churning because of the half-heard story about the body in the fire and because of Tom's infuriating reaction to it. She was in no mood to write or to concentrate on anything at all.

'One phone call,' she thought. *'That's all it takes to put an end to this. I'll tell the police I was there and ask them what information they've given the media, about the victim and so on. One call. I needn't mention Tom.'*

Her argument was seductive but she did nothing about it. For one thing, there was no telephone in the bedroom and a call made downstairs would become a public event. Far easier, she thought, to do it next day when they were travelling. She might pretend she needed to ring Kathy in Yorkshire, and go into a call box, if there was one.

Lifting the curtain, she peered out. The yellowish glow from a ground floor window lit up a few yards of garden, a peat stack and a fence that blurred into the blackness. Linda sighed. Raindrops pattered against the glass. She dropped the curtain.

'It wouldn't be one phone call, would it?' she thought. *'They'd want more than that. And there'd be no way of keeping Tom out of it either.'*

Yet she remained undecided.

She had forgotten to ask him about buying a newspaper in Tarbert and the one in the hotel lounge had no word of the fire. In the morning, she decided, she would make sure she scanned whichever paper was delivered to the hotel. Better, she would make a point of watching the regional television news. The story fascinated her, partly because of its drama but mainly because it was the first time she had been close to a news story.

'Gloucester doesn't count,' she reasoned. *'An outsider might imagine I feel personally involved, but it doesn't touch me. Well, not much. No more than it touches people who have only ever seen the city on their television screens. As far as I can remember, I have never walked down Cromwell Road and I didn't meet the victims or any of the other people in the story. But Dorris Castle is different. I*

was there. Illegally, I was there. And up it went in flames and someone was killed.'

Words stopped forming in her mind. She wrapped her arms around herself for comfort. From what, she wondered. From an arbitrary fate that let her go free while someone else died in the flames?

'Tom's right really,' she thought. *'We haven't anything to say that would be helpful. We didn't see or hear anyone or notice anything that suggested an arsonist was prowling around. Arson? Did anyone mention arson? Tom did. Not the radio, that recited the stock phrase about inquiries continuing into the cause. Well, obviously it's either going to be arson or faulty wiring.'*

Linda remembered the worn old cable that carried power to a sconce-like lamp in a passageway. Old wiring could be dangerous, even fatal. She thought of the tilted lightbulb. In memory, the scene was an accident in preparation.

With a flush of shame she realised that all she would achieve if she telephoned the police was self importance. She had felt embarrassed for those neighbours who had come forward with their sudden revelatory memories once Cromwell Road made the front pages. Why so silent so long when girls were missing, not dead? Sometimes newspaper cheque books were to blame for such timing, but there was a more fundamental reason, a reprehensible need to attach themselves to excitement however horrible.

People quite commonly did that, placing themselves a shade nearer the heart of matters than they had any right to be. By exaggerating their degree of acquaintance with the famous or notorious, or elaborating a non-event into an anecdote designed to leave the listener in no doubt that here was an interesting person, one whose life had been brushed by adventure, in these ways they made their tiny mark. It was not admirable but it was human nature.

And here she was, contemplating the same thing.

Downstairs a door opened and closed. Footsteps mounted the stairs. Linda opened her notebook and pretended to write.

Next morning Tom was gone when she awoke. She expected to find him downstairs, probably poring over the map again, but there was no one in the house except the woman who owned the hotel. She was a sharp featured islander, kinder than she looked. Tom had nicknamed her Mrs Macmuddle because she had mixed them up with some other people and been confused about their booking, and because she had yet another of the Mac names. There seemed to be a preponderance of these.

Mothering Linda, she hoped she had slept well and that her first visit to the islands was enjoyable. Tom, she said, was away walking, having set out early but with the promise to be back for his breakfast. She enunciated carefully, as though the words might bite her.

Linda asked where he had gone. She had to repeat her question and it became apparent that the landlady's difficulty was not that she was muddleheaded but that she found English accents hard to understand.

Mrs Macmuddle pointed to the window, saying: 'He went that way.'

The weather had cleared up overnight. The sun was thin and brilliant and the scenery breathtaking as the islands awoke from the long winter months. It niggled that she had slept on and missed part of it, because of a sleepless night, while Tom who had slept heavily was already out and relishing the day. Then she felt unfair, because the jaunt was a treat for him and it was natural for him to want to take part of this trip down memory lane on his own. She felt niggardly to begrudge him that.

The landlady picked up a frying pan. On the table were a saucepan and a packet of porridge oats. Linda was in the doorway, as close as she could get without going into the kitchen. It did not seem right to be actually in the kitchen. Mrs Macmuddle set the pan down beside the stove, then took a packet of sausages from the fridge and put them next to the pan.

'So you're away to the Dark Island today?'

If Tom had said so, Linda supposed it must be true. She had not heard the name before. 'Yes.'

Before she could add anything, the sausages were abandoned and Mrs Macmuddle was taking a long stride up the room towards her. Her arm was stuck out, her hand clawed. Linda was momentarily alarmed but the woman was not making for the doorway, she was reaching for a television set on a shelf just out of Linda's sight but close inside the door.

'The news,' said Mrs Macmuddle.

Linda forgot about encroaching and went into the kitchen. Conveniently, Mrs Macmuddle favoured the regional news. The fire was soon mentioned. A photograph of a chubby young woman with shoulder length hair filled the screen.

The newsreader said: 'The missing Strathblane secretary, Anita

83

Gayner, has been identified as the woman whose remains were found in Dorris Castle which was damaged by fire on Tuesday.'

'Och, no,' sighed Mrs Macmuddle, and made Linda miss the next bit.

Linda picked it up again when the screen was full of burned tower. She glimpsed the fountain where she had joyfully cleaned her teeth. Within a few yards of that, the missing secretary met her death.

'It is a strange thing,' said Mrs Macmuddle once the news was over and the volume turned down to nothing again, 'to go from your home in Strathblane two years ago and be found dead in that castle.'

Linda murmured agreement. A dob of fat was slipped into the pan, the sausages were being unwrapped. She stayed where she was, retreat seeming as awkward as entry had once been.

Mrs Macmuddle's fingers closed around a plump sausage and flopped it into the pan. 'I believe it is too close. It is not what you would expect, now is it?'

Fascinated by the journey of the next pale sausage from paper wrapper to pan, Linda did not answer. The map in her head was hopeless. She had no idea where Strathblane was, how could she measure the distance to the castle?

'You see,' said Mrs Macmuddle, and she may well have been talking to herself, 'when a young woman packs and goes you expect she is in Glasgow or Edinburgh or away over the border. What are we to make of this? She was only a few miles away. What was she doing for the last two years, with her photo in the papers but no one recognising her? Was she hiding in that old castle all the time?'

Smoke rose from the pan. Six sausages were in there by now. Rashers of bacon were lined up ready and several eggs stood beside a basin and a whisk. Jiggling the pan to prevent the sausages sticking, she spared a glance for Linda. 'I think, perhaps, there is something we are not yet being told about this Anita Gayner.'

Then she turned the heat low under the pan, brought a kettle back to the boil and made tea. Linda preceded her into the dining room and sat, alone, awaiting Tom and mulling over Mrs Macmuddle's analysis of the news story.

'She has a point,' she thought. *'If the woman was in the papers, probably on posters too, she'd have been discovered if she'd stayed in the area. I wonder whether she'd been away and was actually on her way home. But then why stop off at the castle? It's empty, it's not as though anyone lives there. Not for – how long did Tom say*

it had been for sale? More than a year, anyway. Maybe Mrs M's right. Perhaps there is more to it than meets the eye.'

Half way through her cup of tea she had the idea that the surest way of reaching the truth was to make that telephone call. A swap, if you like: I'll tell you my news if you tell me yours. But the police would not do that, she decided. They would hear what she had to say but they would tell her nothing in exchange.

Tom came. He had barely time to greet her with a cheerful: 'You've slept through the best of the day, you know, Maggie,' before Mrs Macmuddle hurried over with their porridge.

'Was it an enjoyable walk?' she asked, setting the bowls in front of them.

He said that indeed it had been. 'I went further than I intended. It's a wonderful day.' He winked at Linda. 'Only the promise of a good breakfast brought me back.'

He was tousled, flushed with exertion, more attractive than in his calmer moods. Linda could see through to the boy who had spent his summers creating adventures in the open air, in a southern sea-side town or on a Scottish island. Her imaginary pictures of the London flat had grown indistinct and unconvincing. He had said nothing to support them and anyway she had only known the gipsy in him.

7

The woman sat like a hermit in her cell, contemplating a world beyond reach. Tides had ebbed and flowed, shadows had stretched and shrunk, but no boats had sailed into view. With bitter resignation she feared another captive night.

He had lied to her, which is what he had done before and what she had come to expect of him. It was no help, believing that. She tried not to but she had long ago run out of plausible explanations for his failure to return. By now she thought of it as his desertion. That was no help either.

She picked over the exact words he had used in his note. But they were no longer his exact words. They had become confused with her previous attempts to recall them and, instead of providing snatches of encouragement, the brief message was reduced to a word game to while away her time. Her memory was as untrustworthy as his promise.

In a flood of self-pity she pictured herself left to rot in this cellar because she had carelessly let him guess her suspicions. She soaked one of her precious paper tissues with her tears before she was able to turn pathos into anger and stop crying and concentrate on ways of surviving.

Careful not to tear it, she spread the tissue on the shelf to dry so that she would be able to use it again. There was so very little, everything must be eked out. The peppermints were frighteningly low, even though she was strict about apportioning them.

As she turned to go to the window, she felt faint. For an instant the walls trembled and leaned in on her. She groped for the shelf and sank down, resting there until she felt stable. The nails fixed in the wall opposite seemed to slide around for a moment and then they were steady too. She wondered whether any of it was real, the effect of an earth tremor say. Once, in Cornwall, she had experienced one. Things had quivered and made her dizzy.

With a wild flight of imagination she saw the sea in turmoil, an upheaval of the land, the cellar ripped apart. Laughing, she tried to say: 'And with one bound she was free!' But her tongue was thick and refused to form the words, and the laugh was an unpleasant growl. Swallowing, moistening her lips with her tongue, she started up the argument about whether to have another piece of peppermint.

Going to the window she looked at the nearest rocks, the ones that were always visible in part, whatever the state of the tide. These rocks were her clock. Sometimes she went by the length of the shadow they threw but at times like this, when it was cloudy, she looked at the water level. One of her markers was a ridge which was now clear of the water by about eighteen inches. She settled that as soon as it was submerged she would eat half a peppermint. Then she made an effort to keep her mind off the peppermints, knowing that if she failed she would either cheat and eat half a sweet before the time was up or else she would be inventing excuses to seek out and nibble crumbs from the packet. In a way, licking crumbs was the worst thing she could do. It kept her mind riveted by the packet of peppermints and relieved neither thirst nor hunger. Besides, it involved cheating because there *were* no crumbs, not unless she created them while pretending to herself she was searching for them.

Scanning the scene outside for anything of interest – a bigger than usual wave; clouds throwing patterns on the water; a glint of metal as a car took a bend on a road; a curious piece of flotsam; a bird doing something slightly different with the carcase of the sheep – she flicked occasional glances at the ridge on the rocks. But for the most part she let the rhythm of the surf lull her, her mind drift as aimlessly as a gull riding the swell.

Every so often she dragged her thoughts back to ways of getting free. Fanciful ways, impossible ways, none were of any practical use. The room was solid, she had no tools and her strength was waning. The conclusion was always the same: help must come from outside. All she could do was keep her spirits up, be sensible about the peppermints and, whenever one of the frequent showers began, hold her tin through the bars to catch a few drops to drink.

Scrabbling around in her memory she thought about other people who, in fiction and in life, had been famously incarcerated. She wished she knew better how they had survived. The religious, naturally, had passed the time in prayer. Some people had exercised to ensure physical fitness. A lot of meditating had gone on.

But none of them had endured the same torture as hers. If they were in official prisons or being held hostage, then they were fed and watered, however meagre and unpalatable the fare. People knew where they were and the prisoners knew that efforts were being made to extricate them. Her predicament was that the only person who knew she was in the country had abandoned her, and that if no one discovered her by accident she would die of starvation.

Cross to have circled to the black thought, she swung her gaze to the ridge on the rock. Half way there. She sighed, stood up and walked about the room, the idea of physical exercise appealing but not very practical. Gentle floor exercises might be beneficial but anything physically demanding was out. She was low on energy, permanently cold and her shoulder was sore.

Back to the window. Water a fraction nearer the ridge. No boats.

A gull sliced in front of the window and landed on the dead sheep. It stepped daintily along the animal's back and then hopped on to the beach and strutted around. All at once she had a plan: attract a gull and attach a message to its leg. True, it was not as good as a homing pigeon but it was a chance. Someone was bound to spot it because the gulls went to and fro between the islands all day. They were not confined, restricted, penned, trapped. They went where they liked and quite often they chose to go off in the direction of the harbour. Before long someone would notice the message and then, then at last, a boat would come for her.

Bread. She had no bread and bread was perfect for attracting gulls. A peppermint? No, not if there was an alternative. Peppermints were her last resort. Shreds of paper tissue then, cast out of the window. White fluttering fragments might look sufficiently like bread for a gull to approach and investigate. Then she would . . . What? Well, grab the bird through the bars, stick the note on its leg. How? Well . . . She brooded on the problem of attaching the note. The ideal, or so she supposed, was a rubber band but she did not have one. In lieu of a rubber band she needed to tie the note on to the leg. But she had no shoe laces or string, nothing to tie with. Wait, though. Hair, of course there was always hair. She felt her scalp, ran fingers down her long hair. Excellent, that was one problem solved. Strands or plaited for extra strength? Setting that decision aside she concentrated on the message.

Thé peppermint wrapper was perfect. It was white and she had not ripped it and made it scrappy. All she need do was empty the sweets into her pocket, flatten out the wrapper and write her message on the inside.

And that is where she stuck. She had nothing to write with.

Water inched up the rocks. A shaft of gold thrust through clouds but then the sun quickly withdrew. Weed writhed in the shallows until a bold wave flung it ashore. All the while she worried how to write her message. There was nothing she could utilise as a nib, no ink but her own blood.

For a long time she experimented with the tin but gouging the ceiling had damaged the corners and although she tried twisting and flattening it, it was impossible to achieve a sharp point. After that she dreamed up several ideas but none she could put into practice. For instance, if her trousers had a belt, she could have used the prong on the buckle. If she had not filed her nails, as a way of passing time on the first day, she might have managed with a bitten off piece of nail. If the rock wall was friable, a shard would have been handy. And if she did not care about keeping the emery board intact, she might have snapped that, but she was reluctant to damage it. She had so few possessions, she hated to lose anything.

When every ingenious idea came to nought, she experimented with a peppermint, snapping it to make an edge and using spit for ink. With no paper to spare, she stroked the letters on the palm of her hand. If it worked, she meant to do a version in blood on the sweet wrapper. But the sweet was the wrong tool. The edge dissolved and she had to snap the peppermint again to make another edge, and so on, over and over until the sweet was all powder and crumbs.

The words, she decided, were wrong. There were too many of them. Her message must be a model of concision, then perhaps she could write it without wasting another peppermint. Because that was what that attempt had amounted to, a sticky hand and a wasted peppermint.

She sat at the window and sucked the sweetness from her skin. The ledge of rock had been swallowed by the sea but there was no reward owed to her for waiting. In crumbs and in licks she had consumed the sweet already.

Sighing, she pushed away a tide of misery. Her world was reduced to a barren room and fussing over a packet of sweets. No, a quarter

of a packet. She gave a bitter smile at the pernickety correction, it exemplified the narrowness of her life now.

Shifting to her knees, she fixed her gaze on the far shore and her mind on the precise wording of the note to send, if only it were possible. It was becoming hard to keep her mind on things. That was partly what had gone wrong with the peppermint experiment, she had muddled the message and made it longer than need be. Another thing, which had flickered briefly through her mind while she was bent on shaping sticky letters, now loomed large. Her message needed to be exact and yet she did not know the name of the island where she was trapped.

He had never given it a name. During their early days together it had passed simply as 'an island' that he knew. Later he had pointed at it from the road, saying it was one among a cluster not too far out in the sound from the main island. But he had never named it. Neither did she know what the group of islands was called. If she had heard the word she could have tried a phonetic rendering of the Gaelic name, but she had no recollection of ever hearing it.

And all that time she had spent with the map, she had been teaching herself the names of the important islands and their sequence down the archipelago: Lewis and Harris, North Uist, Benbecula, South Uist, and Barra. She knew where to slot in some of the smaller ones such as Vatersay and Eriskay. And she was confident that the shapely mountain guarding the western approach to the sound was on Pabbay, and that the island south of it was Berneray, and that both names were to be treated with caution because these islands had namesakes south of Barra.

Yet she had no idea whatsoever of the name of the island where he had made her prisoner.

Her mind wandered again, to windows and those other people who had stared from their cells at worlds beyond their call. Window, the word interested her. A Scandinavian sound about it, perhaps it came from Norse. What was that phrase? *Windows of heaven*, yes, that was it. A medieval concept, she seemed to remember, a belief that the rain fell to earth through windows in the sky. Window might after all be Middle English. Another phrase came to her: *The eyes are the windows of the mind*. Who was she quoting now? She pictured the words on a page, pictured them enhanced with 'e's – *windowes* and *minde*.

If she were right about those 'e's, then it was another old idea. That did not make it any truer than the holes in the sky. Some

people's eyes did not let you see into their souls. You could read their expressions but it was fiction you were reading. He had practised sorcery of that kind, tricking her with kindness and humour and a smile in his eyes. She could not think of a single failure to meet her eye, nor a secretive gleam that might have warned her off. His eyes had misled her as surely as his words and his warmth. He had instructed them to deceive. They were not the windows of his mind.

On the verge of thinking the black thought again, she drew back. She thought about waiting, wearying waiting but also optimistic and joyful waiting like the gap between the decision to become pregnant and the realisation that it had happened, and next the long wait that was pregnancy. Her soon to be ex-husband had not wanted children and she had never taken the decision, babies were among the events she had assumed lay in her future. But her future had shrunk to the space between peppermints, the ins and outs of the sea, the shining of the sun and the dying of the light.

There it was again, the lurch of self-pity she was determined to fight. Too soon, far too soon to indulge in morbidity. Think about those people who endured weeks and months of wretchedness, doubting whether they would come out alive, and yet they had triumphed. Think about them and match their courage, don't give in after only . . . But she did not know how many days and nights she had suffered. Time had blurred because it was not clock time and radio news time signalled by expert measurers of time. She was living on a different scale, her life ruled by the sun and the moon and the stars.

Windows. It popped into her mind that there was a newer kind she had overlooked. People who knew about computers knew about this sort. He would have been very familiar with them although they had not talked about computer technology. He was the owner, or former owner, of a company selling hardware. Or maybe not, maybe none of that was true. He had said it, quite definitely, her mind was not slipping. It was just that what he said might not have been true. She shrugged. Anyway, they had not talked about windows.

There was, she remembered, modern jargon to set alongside the old poetic ideas about windows. Once upon a time not so very long ago someone had tried out a fancy phrase: *window of opportunity*. An elaborate way of saying time or opportunity, but it caught on until at one stage it was impossible for people in business to speak

without using it. She remembered the men at the hotel, bandying business cliches all through dinner. Perhaps neither of them could converse normally, perhaps they went home to their wives and children and spotted windows of opportunity for taking the dog for a walk.

She yawned. Although she had slept, and more frequently than she intended, there was no comfort lying on a stone floor or sitting on the shelf with her head resting against the wall of rock. Each time she woke with cramped muscles and aching bones. Sleeping gave her mind rest but not her body. She wriggled stiff shoulders, felt the twinge where she had yanked the left one as the seat belt tightened and the car slewed into the collision.

In a perfect world, she thought, she would now be taking tea in her flat in the crooked alley, or in the room at the back of Jerome's bookshop, or with her neighbour the jeweller. Oddly, the teapot she imagined herself pouring from at home was not one she owned. It took her a moment to notice that and longer to place it because it was a teapot she had not spared a thought for in twenty years. Her mother had pursued it across half the country. That was another category of waiting: dedicated waiting.

Quite why her mother was besotted with teapots, no one could say. That it was an obsession, no one could doubt. From an inclination to fill shelves on an accidentally acquired dresser, it developed into an urge to possess. Jumble sales, department stores, porcelain dealers' shops – they were all explored for treasure in the shape of teapots. Of course, many of these teapots were scarcely what the average person would call teapot-shaped, but no matter. A handle of sorts and a spout, albeit inefficient at pouring, and the article found favour at 16 The Elms. No 14 collected treen, small decorative items made of wood. No 12 was hot for ribbon plates. Perhaps that was an oblique explanation of the teapots.

Every few months, or so it seemed in memory, a man was called in to tack another shelf along a wall because the pots had multiplied. Several were fun and worth the new shelf, like the monkey pot. His tail was the handle, he sat hugging a nut whose stalk was the spout. Unless her mother had been fooled it was a good one, claimed to be majolica from Minton and made in the 1870s.

But the one in the daydream was not eccentric even though her mother's efforts to get it were. This pot ought by rights, her mother had remarked in a thin-lipped way after a family funeral, to be hers, it had been promised to her. Alas, an aunt was first to sift the nicknacks for a memento and what she chose to keep was the pot. Hints did not prevail, outright requests were out of the question, but the aunt was treated to many more visits than she had merited prior to this. When she sold up and went to live with her son, she gave the pot to her sister. The sister then received the visits. In this way the teapot was pursued around England and around the family for years. Eventually persistence paid off. A cheap Coalport copy, said a man with a monocle in a shop in Kensington Church Street, and left her convinced it was pure Rockingham.

Gulls pirouetted outside the window before gliding coolly out to sea. She did not stir to entice one. The message and the rescue were confined to dreams, she could not make them real.

Far out a slick of darkness was riding the swell. Restless waders patrolled the beach. A breeze puffed the stink of the decaying sheep landward. She jerked away from the window but the smell of death was in the room with her.

She focused her mind on the teapots, a harmless topic fixed in the past. But the comic monkey and the chase for the pseudo Rockingham had been told and she took up the story on the day she came home from school and found a shelf running along her bedroom wall. Teapots were encroaching on the only space in all the world that could be called her own. There had been a terrible row, a screaming match, and her mother had won. Lying in bed after the triumph of the teapots she used to count their ghostly shapes. The numbers grew, there was no curbing them. She fantasised about smashing one, or better than that loosening the screws in the shelf and smashing them all. But she did not try it because the market stalls and shops of the nation were stocked with replacements. All she would achieve was an intemperate buying spree. So she grew used to them, although never used to the spurt of anger each time she entered what was supposed to be her room and discovered yet another interloper.

Afraid of missing something crucial she braved the smell and edged to the window. Just as she got there she heard a sound. A bump. She pictured a boat at the jetty, coming alongside clumsily, caught by a pushy little wave and thudded against the stone. Squashing into the recess she struggled to see the jetty, knowing it was impossible from that angle but guided by instinct. Another bump, followed by a scraping sound of something sliding on stone. Footsteps! She sprang away from the window, head thrown back, eyes on the ceiling. Yes! There it was again, a footstep overhead. She shouted. 'Help! I'm down here. In the cellar. Help! Help! Help!'

Her voice was out of practice, to her own ears she made the sound of a crow. But no matter, she was shouting, she was imploring someone to help her and they would hear this time because they were close. A layer of plaster and perhaps wooden boards was all that separated her from rescue. 'Help! Help! Help!'

Over excited she heard her yells turn to hysterical laughter. The cell threw the noise back at her, frightening her with the animal nature of her cries. She shut up.

There was a long pause before the next sound. A footstep on stone in the kitchen, she was reasoning it out. The kitchen floor was stone and the noise was being made by someone moving around in the kitchen. It appalled her to think she might be out of earshot. The building was solid, wrapped around rock. There was a lobby and a flight of stairs between the kitchen and the cellar, maybe it was the difference between being saved and going unheard. But no, not with the amount of racket she had been making. She took a deep breath and began shouting again.

After every few shrieks she paused and waited for a reply. Like playing with an echo, she thought, like the time she had been with him in the mountains and he had made her shout but her voice had not come back.

There was no responding voice this time either. Grabbing the tin she clanged it on the cellar door, begging to be let out. In the pauses she heard someone blundering about the kitchen, bumping into things. It seemed a chair was knocked over. Then there was a crash as something fell and rolled over the stone flags. The tin of meatballs, she guessed. Someone had stupidly knocked it off the table and it was rolling about on the floor. Perhaps they were drunk. Could that be it? How else could they be so blundering and ignorant that she was there?

And then the chilling thought. Perhaps they knew.

He had come back then, when her sentry duty at the window was between shifts, and now he was making sure she knew he was there and that he was not willing to free her. He was taunting her, trying to drive her mad. Or perhaps he had not left the island. Perhaps he had been there all along, camping in the ruin on the other side of the hill.

From directly overhead, in the bedroom, there came softer sounds. Feet on rugs. She could remember the floor now: wooden boards covered with rugs. Again she clamoured at the door, begging him, cursing him, mouthing wordless anguish until she was exhausted.

When she broke off the noises upstairs had also stopped. She listened a long while, for the time it took the sea to deliver a skein of weed to the surf, and for the surf to throw it on the beach where it coiled like a shining noose.

Racked by despair she let the tears wash over her face. Gradually she came round to thinking she had been wrong, he had not been in the house tormenting her or hiding out in the ruin for days. It was a short step to deciding she had imagined the entire episode, that she might be on the way to madness.

Worn out she slumped against the wall and shut her eyes. Sleep had almost overtaken her when there was a faint sound from the beach. Opening one lazy eye she watched a ram ambling away from the house.

Sensitised to sound, each slight movement outside woke her. The swish of the surf was no longer lulling but a call to look, yet when she looked there was nothing significant to see. Birds and water, a dead sheep and now a live one, that was all. She got to her feet, stretched, rubbed painful joints and warmed herself up by pacing.

8

'The Dark Island?' said Tom. 'You want to go there, do you?'

'No, no, this is your treat. We go wherever you fancy. It's just that Mrs Macmuddle understood from you that that's where we were heading.'

She congratulated herself on sounding relaxed. A couple of days of playing at being light-hearted and then, once he had guided her back to her car, she would be free to leave him.

He sighed over the landlady's confusion. 'We talked about the place, but I didn't say that.'

'What is it anyway? It doesn't sound particularly Scottish.'

'The real name's Benbecula. Locally it's often known as the Dark Island, although strictly, I suppose, it isn't an island any more because it's linked by causeways to North Uist and South Uist.'

He challenged her with a sideways look and she pulled a face at him. He was testing her by tossing out the names, but she passed the test. She too had pored over Mrs Macmuddle's map, as well as the one in the hire car, and she had a fair grasp of the geography of the archipelago.

'That's quite a long way from here,' she said, hinting at the extent of her knowledge.

They were travelling down the eastern seaboard where the sea fingered the land. Villages had grown up at the tip of each finger. Linda admitted she was surprised by the gentleness of the landscape and the apparent prosperity.

'Enjoy it while you have the chance,' said Tom.

And she understood that the rest would be what one expected of the isles: harsh and rocky and crabbed by the wind; nettled graveyards with stones worn to illegibility.

He said: 'They call this the golden road because of what it cost when they built it in the thirties.'

96

'The nineteen thirties?'

'Oh yes, they had nothing like this until then.'

He was in a good mood, chatty, which made her play acting easier. Before very long her interest in the journey was genuine. The road wriggled on, around each bay or inlet and between the tiny fresh water lakes, the lochans, that polka-dotted the land. She mouthed silently the splendid names of pre-Cambrian rocks, words she had culled from the guidebook's half page of geology, stone words. Amphibolite. Pegamatite. She cherished them, the first sounding appropriately like something rearing out of the sea, and then the clipped precision of the other. The pair of them, dark masses of amphibolite and coarsely crystalline veins of pegamatite, formed the archipelago. Archipelago was a fine word too.

Tom quoted a line from her taped poem, the one about 'the blue and airy days'. He used it as a label for the morning, and the using of it was a compliment. But although her phrases were apt, she had lost confidence in the poem and wished he would not pick up bits of it and hold them out for inspection, which he did from time to time.

'Insignificant choices, that's what I was referring to,' she said in reply. It was untrue, she had begun to put that slant on it recently. 'It's about all those hardly thought about decisions that make one life different from another.' She wondered whether she ought to rework the poem along those lines.

'From all others?'

'Quite. From all others.'

He tried another line on her, about truth and loyalty.

Linda wriggled her shoulders, discouraging him. 'Don't, Tom.'

'You've gone off it?'

'Maybe. I don't know. I don't want it recited at me.'

'But you thought it was so clever you brought a tape of it on holiday with you.'

'Not to listen to it, you know that wasn't why.'

'Oh come on, what else?'

'To spur me on to write something different. To remind me what I had once been, or been on the verge of being. I didn't plan to hear it over and over.'

'A pity we've left it in your car.'

'Oh no it isn't.'

'Recite me the new one.'

'There isn't one.'

'There must be, you've been shutting yourself away and writing it. Say it to me.'

'No, really, there isn't anything yet.'

'Just a verse.'

'No.'

'A line or two.'

'No.'

'One line, just one.'

'I can't.'

'You mean won't.'

'Both,' she said. 'I won't and anyway I can't.'

With mock gravity he said: 'You are not destined to be a great poet. Face it, your rate of production is against you.'

'And whose fault is it if I'm stuck? Who's been distracting me?'

'Stuck? Is this the famous writer's block?'

'If I were a famous writer, it might be.'

'Then we must find you a perfect quiet place to write. No interruptions, no distractions, just you and your muse.'

Linda laughed. 'Then stop the car, anywhere will do.'

'Anywhere on the golden road? No, you'd make excuses to hop on a bus or hitch a lift to the bright lights of Tarbert. Not here, Maggie. We can do better than this.'

'We're not going to do it at all. We're tracking down your childhood haunts, Tom, that's why we're here. You mustn't let me and my poetry spoil that for you.'

He tweaked a strand of her hair and did not appear to mind.

Tom filled the morning with laughter and lightness. He teased and provoked and let her get away with nothing. She was content to let him win the tussles and confident that she would be able to go on burying her doubts about him until the trip to the islands was over. Another day or two, that was all. She could do it, she was determined to.

They kept to the gentler side of the island, the east, with its golden road, its hamlets and pools of sky, and always the islands lying like basking whales. Occasionally they saw people but not many and not often. Tom started some of his nonsense about it being the end of the world, the promised land where there was peace and solitude and space.

'Promised land? Who promised?' she asked with a dash of irony.

'*I* promised. Remember? When you wanted to imitate the American road movies.'

'And books. Yes, I remember.'

So long ago, in one way. So very few days in reality, less than her allotted fortnight. The days had flown past, crammed with small decisions about where to stay, what to eat and which direction to take next. Each choice they had made had carried them further and further from their regular lives and into the northern emptiness. For him it was a homecoming of sorts, a re-encounter with childhood. For her it had been, mostly, fun. And now that it was not, now that she was concealing nagging suspicions, she had discovered a talent for feigning.

Linda wished she could say something to him about the differences between them, comparing her venturing out with his attempt to go back, an attempt she classed as predictable failure. But she did not speak of the difference. He was being light and amusing her, brimming with that boyish excitement she found touching. It was a glorious morning and they were travelling, it was not a propitious moment for contemplation, reflection, digging beneath the surface of their day to consider what each of them was separately doing.

Later, she thought, probably in the evening over a lazy dinner she would lead him into talking about it. Those were the best times, when an interesting day was ending and they were both tired and content to talk quietly about their lives and their time together, and where they had been and where they were going.

On the edge of her memory was a poem by Herrick, probably by him, she was more or less sure of that. She could not disentangle facts from impressions, but thought the poem was about dream and reality, or maybe about layers of existence. Frowning, she tried to catch the memory but it stayed beyond reach. No doubt it would come clear when she was no longer interested, the way these teasers did.

She had an inkling that the elusive poem connected with the one she was working on herself, the one she had protested was unwritten. She had not been entirely truthful with Tom. It had begun well, foundered and was recovering. Gradually the mists obscuring it were dispelling and she could now say that it was an oblique comment on her strange journey, an exploit during which she denied the truth about her destination, her identity, her home town, and was travelling alongside Tom while knowing they were each taking different journeys.

Linda wondered whether a man who had once quoted Eliot at

her would grasp what her poem meant or whether he would embarrass her by arguing obtusely. Sometimes Tom was one thing, sometimes another.

The car had stopped. He was looking at her, the corners of his mouth curling. She flinched as he snapped his fingers near her face. 'Daydreamer.'

Linda caught the hand and kissed his fingers. 'Nonsense, I was communing with my muse. Isn't that what you require of me?'

She got out of the car and leaned against it. Tom did not although she fully expected him to join her. Regardless, she spoke her words aloud. 'Sky, water, Skye on the skyline. And islands. Islands without number because I am not going to count them, I want to be impressed by their numberlessness.'

'What are you chattering about?'

'Heaven,' she said with an encompassing sweep of her arm.

He smirked. 'I told you you'd like it.'

'Where next?' She was feeling empty. Mrs Macmuddle's breakfast had been a long time ago. Lunchtime was close and they faced the next round of petty decisions, about where and what to eat.

'You're in heaven and you're asking where next? Some people are never satisfied.'

The day was sunshiny but not warm and she was not wearing her jacket. As she opened the car door to get back in she recalled the bag of groceries and worried that he had been serious about picnicking. But it was all right, he was pointing along the coast, saying: 'I thought we'd beg lunch at a bar down there.'

Linda checked the time on the car clock, then turned on the radio. 'We can have the news in a moment,' she said.

Tom groaned and turned it off. 'There's never any new news. It's always the same, you know exactly what it will be.'

She made a quip about the charm of the familiar but the radio remained off.

In a few moments she caught the sweet reek of peat smoke from a chimney, and soon they were in the bar. While pies were being heated and beer poured, she read a newspaper. Anita Gayner's photograph was on the front page, the same shot that had been on television the previous evening. Linda's jaw tightened, and all the tension she had worked to dispel during the drive came flooding back. Tom gave a warning scowl when she was about to remark on it. Instead she handed him the paper and let him see for himself.

His precaution seemed excessive. Half Scotland was discussing the finding of the body, what would it matter if she and Tom did? But he was determined not to let anyone know they had a special interest in Dorris Castle and events there. At breakfast, when she had started to tell him what she had learned from Mrs Macmuddle's television, he had hushed her. Up in their room, packing to leave, he had been adamant she should not refer to it in public.

He had said: 'Things stick in people's minds. You never know who's listening or what they will make of it. Safer to say nothing.'

His voice had been a whisper. She had whispered back, ironically, asking him whether it would be all right if she were to mention the matter to him. So he had heard her out as she recited the news story and followed up with Mrs Macmuddle's opinion. Then he had shaken his head, apparently at a loss to know what to make of either the original story or the Macmuddle contribution.

Linda had forgiven him for not sharing her alarm when she first heard about the body, and she was not surprised by his disinclination to theorise about Anita Gayner's whereabouts for her two missing years, but she had refused to quash her own interest.

'You must admit,' she had said, knowing he would do no such thing, 'that it's intriguing.'

In the bar that lunchtime her eyes kept straying to the newspaper. After reading it Tom had flopped it down on the table next to theirs, well away from her.

'*Another precaution,*' she thought. '*Making sure I don't pore over it and draw attention to us.*'

It was laughable, they were the only customers and the barman had gone away and left them quite alone. But to retrieve the paper she would have to rise from her chair and walk past Tom, or else ask him to return it to her. Doing either would annoy him and then the bright mood of the morning would be tarnished. It was not worth it.

Tom was telling her more about the islands, not quizzing her on her own knowledge this time but showing off his. Although her interest was genuine, she could not prevent her gaze falling again on the newspaper. He had folded it open on page six and folded it in half. As he turned to her, she raised her eyes to the clock on the wall.

Fooled, he said: 'That's not working. It's about an hour later.'

She made a show of comparing her watch with his and adjusting it, although she believed hers to be the more accurate of the two. Not for the first time, she felt like a woman indulging a child, performing an act that was unnecessary in itself but was calculated to please. Presumably Tom did not notice, presumably children did not.

Linda was still puzzled how she had slipped into agreeing to visit the islands, but there was only another day or two to go and she was resolved to be indulgent for that long. She did not like having to humour him, which was tantamount to taking on the responsibility for someone else's unpredictable temperament, and that was a ludicrous situation to get into. Until she was reunited with her own car and could say goodbye and head south, she had no option but to make the best of it. The best was good, like this morning, with her playing the ardent tourist and Tom being entertaining. Two more days, she decided, was manageable.

In a while Tom went to find the toilets, through a door in the wall beneath the clock. Two seconds later Linda shot from her seat and began fumbling with the newspaper, pulling out the front and back pages and leaving the rest looking exactly as it had been, page six on view.

Anxious not to be caught reading it again, she folded the sheet until it fitted into the zipped pocket inside her jacket. Then she sat down and hoped there was no evidence she had moved. Immediately he came back she was going to suggest they drive on while the sunshine lasted. A front of cloud was visible far to the west. Meanwhile, she sat there feeling like the thief she was.

Soon she heard Tom talking to the barman. Their conversation seemed interminable. Having snatched the pages, she was anxious to be gone before she was discovered, but Tom was idling. She thought about hurrying him up, by interrupting with a warning about the threatened change in the weather, but before she had made up her mind he pushed open the door and called her.

'Maggie, come and see this.'

In a store room beyond the bar a collie bitch lay suckling a cluster of damp new puppies. The barman was prideful, the bitch wary, and Tom was telling a story about having owned a collie puppy when he was a boy. Linda knew at once that he was lying.

'So he's doing it too,' she thought. 'Indulging, humouring, saying what fits and keeps people happy.'

Then she had a second thought, that Tom was not doing the same as she was. 'He's doing it for himself, not for me or the barman. We wouldn't have become bad tempered if the lie hadn't been told. Tom's romancing about his childhood again. That's all.'

She disguised her certainty about the lie. 'What did you call your puppy?'

'Scotty. I wasn't very imaginative, I'm afraid.'

Linda asked the barman whether it would be easy to find homes for all the litter. There were about half a dozen. It was impossible to be exact because of the way they were lying, the tiny bodies overlapping each other or half-buried in the mother's fur.

A regretful shake of the head. 'It will be a sad task but we can't let her keep them all.'

A sad task. His words were accompanied by a gesture, a pushing away. The sad task was killing.

Tom said: 'I saw that once when I was a boy. At a neighbour's house. She showed me the puppies when they were new and I wanted to see them again so I went back. She didn't know I was there and I saw her drowning them, taking them up one by one and holding them under the water, and when it was over, flinging them into a bucket, all soggy and dead.'

There was an awkward pause. Linda noticed how his face had tightened. She had no doubts about this memory, the pain of it scarred his face.

The barman sighed. 'If the Lord would only send them singly instead of by the half dozen.'

Then the bitch stirred and some of the puppies fell from her teats, and there was a shuffling about as the animals rearranged themselves. While the barman and Tom were occupied watching them, Linda followed a sign that said toilets.

The folded newspaper felt huge in her pocket. She stood this way and that in front of the mottled mirror above the washbasin, trying to convince herself that the line of the jacket was not altered. Perhaps, she thought, she ought to tear off the unwanted back page, then the wad of paper would be only half as thick. But she did not want to spend time on it, it was more important to get Tom into the car and away before the pages were missed.

Emerging, she could not find anyone. She put her head into the store room, drawing a low growl from the collie, and then pushed open the door to the bar. Empty. Her eye went to the table where the newspaper had been lying. It was no longer there. She scanned the other tables, the bar top and the shelf below the optics. No paper.

Linda rushed outside. Tom was near the car. There was no sign of the barman. She made her remark about the weather.

He looked west. 'We'll be all right for three hours yet.'

'With that lot hanging around?' The whipped up piles of cloud filled most of the western sky.

He tipped his head in the direction of the bar. 'I've been taking local advice and I'm promised those clouds will hold off for three hours. Then, of course, they will charge at us.'

Linda got into the passenger seat, her glance flickering over the interior and checking for a glimpse of the newspaper. She was desperate to know which of them had taken it, Tom or the barman. If it were Tom, then the sooner she knew the better.

As she fastened her seatbelt, she felt the folded pages shift inside her pocket. She was afraid they had rustled and he had heard them and he would . . .

In her head an exasperated voice yelled at her. *'Stop it! You're being ridiculous. You took a sheet of a newspaper, it wasn't honest but it isn't a terrible crime, either. If he knows you've got it he'll be annoyed you're dwelling on the fire, and he'll be grumpy. But that's all. Why on earth are you getting into such a state about it?'*

And then she went back to thinking that it was two days more, that was all. Two days and they would be back on the ferry, back to her car, back to her being free to go where she wanted, and free of Tom too. Two days.

Banks of cloud hung like a warning in the sky as Tom followed the coast road north-west. After a few miles he pulled up, she supposed to admire the scenery without risking driving off the road. The sound was peppered with miniature islands. Further out lay bigger ones, rimmed with creamy sand, the summits of their mountains capped with snow. Reefs jutted from the water, sharp as teeth ready to tear the keel from a boat. Headlands lazed like dragons.

Tom said: 'That's where I used to go.'

His finger traced a route across the water to a cluster of greenish rocky humps riding the sea. She was relieved that they lay close inshore.

She had taken up play acting again, pretending to be fascinated by his memories of the islands and nothing darker. 'I wonder how much is left of it, the house you say was not much better than a shed.'

Expecting him to become disappointed, she was afraid he might turn it against her.

He said they were reasonably strong, those old places. 'They had to be tough. Of course it's still there, it's bound to be.'

With a wry look she discouraged optimism. 'Well, let's hope so.'

'We'll know soon.'

She raised an eyebrow. 'You're not planning to go there today, surely.'

'Why not? The weather's perfect.'

'Yes, but . . .'

'You have to catch it while you can. I told you, I tried a few years ago and it was impossible to cross. I'm not going to risk missing it again, not now that we've come all this way.'

She said it was rather late in the day to be thinking about boats and crossings.

Tom turned the ignition key. 'The sooner the better then.'

'Where can we cross from?'

'There.' He pointed to a straggle of buildings some way ahead.

Resigned, she could not resist saying: 'A pity we couldn't go out there one morning though, you'd have heaps of time. As it is, it's going to be a rush.'

She was dreading a return crossing with the clouds upon them and probably the wind and the rain too. Tom, seeming to guess what was in her mind, increased his speed.

They reached the village. Buildings blurred by. He asked her to wait in the car while he arranged for someone to take them across.

Linda encouraged a mean hope that no boat would be available. The cloud front was pressing towards them, shadows were lengthening, and it was the season of short days. If only they could try it next day instead, she thought. Perhaps, if she could tell Tom that fine weather was forecast for the morning . . .

It was coming up to the hour. She turned on the car radio. The international news had gone by and she heard the end of the British news. There was more horror from Cromwell Road, Gloucester. Another Gloucester story too: an elderly jeweller had died of a heart attack after youths had raided his shop near the cathedral. The archdeacon had been a witness. Three youths were to appear in court.

Shocked numb for a moment, she recovered with a bitter cry, not words just outrage. There was no mistake, she had heard his name. Arnold Wilkins.

She pictured him beckoning her into the shop, and the marcasite brooch twinkling up at them from the display cabinet where he set the teacups.

'Is that what they killed him for?' she demanded as anger seized hold of her. 'Did they grab the marcasite bow and those useless charms no one wanted to buy? Is that what they were after, cheap stock he couldn't sell?'

Then she remembered him in her flat, on his only visit, becoming party to her deception. Yes, he would deliver the faked postcard to Helen and Rusty and Jerome at the bookshop. Yes, he would help her.

Her mind skipped to another postcard, the real one she had sent him from the north of England, the one with the cunning message that hinted at their collusion. Counting days, she wished she could be certain it had reached him. Suddenly she could not bear the idea that he had died without receiving it, without knowing that she was thinking about him. She burst into tears.

Tom appeared in the driver's seat beside her. 'What the hell's the matter?'

'Mr Wilkins. The jeweller. He's dead. It was on the radio.'

'Killed?' He explained the abrupt assumption. 'I mean, you don't get on the radio if you die naturally do you? Not unless you're terribly famous?'

Nodding vigorously she confirmed it. She was sniffing, sobbing, fighting to control herself. Tom gave her a tuft of paper tissues from the box beneath the dashboard and waited while she blew her nose. Then she told him what she knew, but she did not say exactly what had made her break down because that was a foolish, petty thing.

Tom patted her arm. 'Gloucester, you said.'

For a moment she did not appreciate what he was driving at. Then he said: 'You told me you lived in Bristol. Why did you tell me Bristol?'

Smearing away the last of the tears, she admitted the lie. 'Oh, it was too difficult to say Gloucester. Everybody's talking about that place and I couldn't bear to.'

He was looking at her oddly, with the expression she had noticed on the day she told him about the Italian holiday ruse. 'You said Bristol and it wasn't true.'

She dropped the soggy tissues on the floor of the car by her feet, and swallowed. 'Are you cross about that?'

Slowly he shook his head. He did not look cross, she could not say how he looked. There were secret thoughts that were not reflected in his eyes, and she could not think what they might be.

'As a matter of fact,' he said. 'I knew your jeweller friend lived in Gloucester.'

'*Did* you?'

'You showed me the postcard.'

'Oh, yes.'

And she was back in an English seaside town, sitting in her car on the esplanade while Tom was obligingly dropping the card into a pillar box. She was, she concluded, an incompetent deceiver.

Linda gave a rueful smile. 'Tom, if you knew, why didn't you say anything about it?'

All she got in reply was the wicked look.

Then he dropped the subject and told her about the arrangements for getting to the island. They were to meet a boatman in ten minutes.

Linda stirred herself to take an interest in all this but her heart was at home, in her flat in the crooked alley by the cathedral. She knew the worst but she wished she knew the details too. Had Mr Wilkins been attacked? Had he died immediately or later? Was he alone? What was stolen? Were the culprits any of the people whom she had seen pressing their faces against the window but not entering? Would it have made any difference if she had been at home instead of pretending to be in Italy?

In spite of trying her hardest to share Tom's enthusiasm for the trip, questions about Mr Wilkins' death kept crowding in on her. Tom did not refer to it again. She wondered whether this was deliberate because he feared more tears if they dwelt on the subject, or whether it was possible for him to be as unmoved as he appeared.

In ten minutes they were being raced across the water. The roar of the engine precluded conversation and reduced Linda's communication with the boatman to nods and smiles. He was a young man with a fast boat and the chance to show it off, so he was not concerned about her. For most of the way she sat with her back to him and concocted phrases to describe sunshine glittering in their wake. She anchored her hair efficiently by stuffing it down her collar, and congratulated herself on having withstood Tom's repeated cajoling to have it cropped.

'You'd look different,' he had argued one time, making different sound like an improvement.

'Unrecognisable,' she had laughed. 'My friends wouldn't know me.'

'You say you want to remake your life, and yet you won't risk a haircut. I thought hairstyles were the first things women altered when they wanted a change.'

'Call me perverse,' she had said, and she had not gone near a hairdresser.

The boatman approached the island with great caution. Apparently he had never been there before. He slid up beside a stone jetty and Tom jumped ashore. His eagerness touched Linda's heart. So *this* was the spot where he had whiled away those long ago summers, this place was the highlight of his childhood, and this moment was his longed-for return. She watched him bubbling with energy, with remembered pleasures he was keen to share with her, and she was so very glad she had agreed to come. To indulge someone, to accommodate their wishes and humour them, was not unrewarding.

'Look,' Tom said to her as she stood by him on the jetty, 'I'm going to nose around over that way. Do you want to stay here?'

She floundered. 'I don't know. How long will you be?'

'Five minutes at the outside.'

'Then I'll wait here.'

He was running when he left her, along the jetty, across a rough beach, up a crumbling pathway and over a low headland. For a second he was outlined against the sky and then he dropped out of view. Birds rose beyond the hill, screaming at being disturbed. Linda looked at the boatman, ready to make a joke of it, but the man was busy titivating something in his wheelhouse. He stayed in the boat, rocking against the old stone slabs. Water had gnawed the stones, it was parting them from their neighbours and several had slipped away and lay at odds with the line of the wall.

Tom waved Linda to join him on the beach. His excitement was irrepressible, he hugged her as soon as she reached him.

'Isn't this place fantastic?'

She said she was longing to know what was over the hill.

'You do know.'

'The house?'

But he was on his way to the jetty to speak to the boatman. Linda followed the path over the headland. Once it might have been a neat, safe track but wind and weather had eroded it and she had to watch her footing despite the temptation to stare at the island-dotted sound and the backdrop of mountains. On the top she stood, breathing the sharp air and admiring the clean colours.

The boat was leaving.

She screamed for Tom. 'Tom! The boat. Look, the boat.'

There was no answer.

She waved frantically at the boat, yelling: 'Wait. Come back.' And even as she did so she knew the boatman would not hear her cries or anything but the engine.

Below her on the path there was a movement. Tom's head appeared, hair tangled by the wind.

'Tom, the boat's going.' With a jolt she realised that he knew, that he had sent the boatman away. She had never intended to be in this secret place alone with him. She had been relying on the boatman's presence but Tom had dismissed him.

She grabbed his arm as he came within reach. 'What on earth did you do that for? He was supposed to be taking us back. Now what are we going to do?'

He shook her off, less angry than entertained by her rage.

'We're on an island with a house, we'll be fine.'

She looked wildly round. 'What house? The remains of one that was never better than a shed?'

'You're exaggerating.'

'But . . .'

He walked past her, saying: 'Come on, I'll show you.'

And he went quickly so that she had to stumble along behind him, like a toddler barely keeping up with an adult. The path dipped on the far side of the headland and a few yards further on it forked. Away to the left were stone walls and a curve of roof. The old stone house was as basic and bare as he had said, if not more. Part of its roof had gone and grass encroached where there used to be a floor of stone slabs. There had never been anything fancy about it and now it was being sucked back into the earth.

Again Tom invited her to say how fantastic, how marvellous, how wondrous a place it was. She did try, she did not succeed and his eagerness was transformed into determination to wrest enthusiasm from her.

'You're being a bit half-hearted, aren't you?'

'Sorry, I don't mean to be. It's an incredible place. I mean, to be a child playing here . . . You were extraordinarily lucky.'

'There's never been anywhere better. I know *you* can't appreciate it.'

'Oh, I do. I really think it's terrific. A tiny speck in the sea . . . There's always something special about islands, isn't there?'

'For me, this is the special one. I don't expect you to see it.'

Linda waffled on about the scenery and the pleasures of being on an island, and then about the fictional significance of islands. She cited *The Tempest* and the *Odyssey* as literary examples of islands as new worlds where new rules applied and visitors faced difficulties and had to fall back on their resources. Planets, she said, served the same literary function in science fiction stories. On and on she went, finding it hard to bring it to an end. Worse, she sounded false. Tom's island was mildly interesting, no more than that. He wanted her to convince him she found it extra special but all she could do was treat it as a symbol, a literary device. She was letting him down.

She was very worried about the boat. By this time it was a white dot close to the harbour from which they had set out. She regretted having been so obviously alarmed, because hiring a boat in a world of islands was presumably like hiring a taxi in town. You ordered one and it arrived when you needed it, it did not hang around for hours. She decided not to mention it again as she would see it as soon as it started the outward journey.

'Tell me about the holidays,' she said, being indulgent.

'You've heard most of it.'

'No, come on. Tell me where you slept and how your mother cooked and how you . . .' She almost asked how they had got themselves to and from the main island but that would revive the question of their own return trip and so she sheered away. '. . . how you spent the days.'

Stooping at the low doorway, they entered the house. There was no window, only daylight through the door and the torn away roof.

'Over there,' he said, 'was my bed.'

He pointed out where all the other furniture had stood and described dazzling mornings climbing the hill to cut peat to stack for future fires and afternoons fishing from rocks. None of it was new to her. Once her eyes had adjusted to the gloom, she walked to the end where a black band of soot rose from the hearth to the chimney. There was no stove or grate, only a hearthstone.

'Tough on Tom's mother,' she thought with sarcastic disbelief. *'You'd have to be a hopeless romantic to enjoy cooking on an open fire.'*

For a while she encouraged him to reminisce. It was fair, it was what he had come for. But she was privately amused by the gap between what he said had gone on there and what seemed possible. At one stage he claimed that a cousin and friends stayed there too and it was perfectly plain that they could not all have done so, not at once. The house was a one room shack with a chimney at one end and a door half way down one of the long walls. It was out of the question that all those people had squeezed into it and spent a jolly holiday together for weeks on end.

'*Unreliable memories,*' she thought. '*It wouldn't have been fun, it would have been murder.*'

A breeze blew through the doorway and lifted her hair. Linda glanced around. The sea was a duller blue, the nearest island drabber than it had been. Clouds were moving in.

She stepped outside, saying: 'I'd love to see the rest, Tom.'

She sounded brighter than she felt. She was casting her eye along the shore of the main island seeking the white dot that would mean rescue before the day faded into a cold and wet evening. There was no dot.

'Come on then,' Tom said. He skipped over a frantic stream and held out a hand to catch her as she leaped too. Landing, she crashed against him, and he held her tight and they were laughing.

Her doubts about the weather dispelled as his excitement infused her. There they were on his minute childhood island, a toy island, and she was heady with freedom.

'We can do anything, Tom, we can run and jump and shout and do crazy things and nobody can see us or hear us or tell us to shut up or act grown up.'

When he replied in Caliban's words, '. . . *the isle is full of noises, sounds and sweet airs, that give delight and hurt not* . . .', she burst out laughing because she was supposed to be the poet, she ought to be the one to quote Shakespeare, not Tom.

He was laughing with her. He picked her up and swung her round, and he was laughing. He swung her, and the islands revolved around her, the whole of Scotland spun, the whole earth and the sky. Then he was running, pulling her after him, uphill, up to the highest place, a blue rock, the pinnacle from which they lorded it.

'There ought to be a flag pole,' she said, gasping for breath.

'We'll get one.'

She sank down on her knees. 'And a chair lift and a bar to serve reviving tots of whisky.'

'We'll get them,' he said.

111

Below lay a patch of scalped land where men used to cut peat. A path ran away from it, over the hillside and out of sight. *'On its way to a beach,'* she thought, *'because wherever you go on this island, you're on your way to a beach. No cliffs, thank God, nothing as dangerous as that.'*

Rocks straggled out to sea. 'Was that where you fished, Tom?'

'In good weather, when it was safe.'

'What did you catch?'

'Everything.'

For now, she succumbed. For now, she was willing to believe in his excesses. 'Tell me about the day you caught the shark,' she said, teasing, tempting.

He played her game. 'Oh, you must be bored with that old story.'

'No, come on, I love it.'

Immediately he was inventing a tale, an incredible catalogue of daring and near disaster, with himself strongly featured as young hero. Linda egged him on.

'You've missed out the bit where it swallowed the rowing boat.'

'*Life*boat.'

'Oops, sorry.'

'People on the mainland heard about it and wanted to stuff it and put it in a museum. I could have been famous.'

'But naturally you were modest and wouldn't let them.'

'Oh, it wasn't that. They were too late. We'd eaten it.'

'I can see it now, your mother cooking shark steaks in a pan on the open fire.'

'She was a good cook.'

'She'd need to be.'

'Come on.' And he was dragging her up and they were running again, downhill, fast, too fast for her liking. Memories flashed by, memories of other rough descents like the one on the muddy path below the hillfort on the Welsh border. That was the day she had met him, *really* met him, and her world had shifted off course. She was still unsure what she thought of him, what she felt for him. He was so many different characters: some cheered her, some exhilarated her, some depressed her and some frightened her. None of them bored her.

They slithered to a halt, her heart fluttering like a bird trapped in her rib cage. She flattened her flying hair and straightened her clothes. Then she gave a yelp.

'Oh! I didn't know that was there.'

Close to the shore, yards below them, was another house. A proper one, this time. As they stumbled down to it she saw how it had been built into the hillside, around a rock. Most of it was single storey but by the time it reached the shore it was two. There was a barred window overlooking the beach, and between the bars was a pale shape, a face peeping out. As it moved it became a gull and lifted gently into the air to float away like thistledown.

It did not surprise her when Tom jiggled the door catch and let them in. A man who would spend a night in a spare castle would have no qualms about breaking into this house. Breaking in? Perhaps he would admit it this time, she thought, as he had no key. Anyway, they were in.

There was furniture in all the rooms, linen in a chest, a radio with a nearly flat battery, and a few tins of food in a cupboard. She poked around, not challenging his right to take her there, clear that he had no right. She did not care. The peculiar freedoms of the island made all behaviour acceptable.

Their bags were on the jetty where they had dumped them. They trotted over the beach together to fetch them. The jetty was just out of sight of the house, that was why she had missed seeing the building when they arrived. Bending to lift her bag, she fixed her eyes on the far shoreline, checking whether the boatman was on his way. She did not care much whether he hurried or not. Being on the island was fun, especially since she had discovered that if he let them down there was somewhere dry and reasonably comfortable to sleep.

Tom's bag was heavy because he had pushed the picnic purchases in on top of his clothes. As soon as they were in the kitchen again he lifted out a bottle of whisky, packets, cans and a box of matches.

Linda brought glasses, small tumblers, from a cupboard and attempted to rinse them under the tap but the water was not running.

'We'll have to turn it on outside,' Tom said. 'There's a tap round the back.'

She held the glasses to the light. 'They look clean. I was being fussy because I don't know when they were last used.'

'Not for months. The people who own all this use it for holidays, when the weather's decent. They probably haven't been out here since autumn.'

'Who are they?' She was wiping the glasses on a teatowel.

'People from London. A Scots family but they live in London.

113

The MacTwaddles, somesuch name. They've owned it for years. No one else comes, except for the farmer who keeps a few sheep here and he'll only come once or twice a year.'

Linda put the tumblers on the table and Tom poured whisky. They raised their glasses in a silent toast, to cheek and complicity.

Outside, ribbons of cloud were blowing down the sound. Warmth and lightness were drained from the day. On the main island one or two yellow lights appeared, distant jewels. Linda closed the door and Tom struck matches and lit an oil lamp and a heater. The wick in the lamp was frayed and a dark strand of smoke coiled towards the ceiling.

'A pity,' she said, 'we can't have a peat fire.'

There was peat in a bucket on the hearth, a hand's reach from the wooden table where they were sitting. Succinctly he scotched the idea.

'Smoke. We don't want to advertise we're here.'

'The man who brought us knows.'

'Yes, but . . .'

She waited for him, then pressed him to continue. 'But what, Tom?'

He shook his head, unwilling to say what he had been about to. Instead he drank another inch of his whisky.

Linda watched the unsteady flame in the oil lamp. If it failed they would be in the dark.

'Is there a torch?' she asked.

'I haven't seen one. Why?'

'I was just thinking it's getting dark and when the boatman comes we'll have to go down to the jetty again.'

He regarded her over the rim of his glass. 'There's no need to worry about that.'

'You mean he's sure to have a torch? Well, I suppose he does but . . .'

'He isn't coming.' He was wearing his wicked look.

A twinge of fear tightened her scalp. To play with the notion of staying overnight was one thing, the reality another. She contrived to seem unconcerned. To her own ears she sounded idiotically playful. She was afraid she was close to hysteria. The strain of acting a role all day, coupled with the mounting anxiety since the boatman had left, were bringing her close to breaking point. She was frightened that her sham would collapse, in accusation and recrimination.

But what she said aloud was: 'I know you enjoy escapades, Tom, but isn't this a shade too reckless? How are we going to get off this rock?'

He leaned back on his kitchen chair and crossed his ankles. 'We like it here, why should we want to leave?'

'Because . . .' Because they were intruders and because the freedom of the island was spoiled if she was denied the freedom to leave. But she dried after the first word, reluctant to be the one who justified and explained. She revived her original point: how were they to cross to the main island? When she repeated it, the jokiness was missing.

Tom tried to spin it out but soon saw that she was not prepared to be twisted about. He gave in and answered her question. 'There's a boat here.'

Sceptical, she said she had not seen one.

'I dare say,' he replied, 'but you hadn't noticed this house either.'

'Where is it?'

He jerked a thumb over his shoulder. 'Along that way.'

Ready for trickery, she quizzed him about it. 'Why wasn't it at the jetty? That's where I'd expect a boat to be.'

'The MacTwaddles keep it where they keep it, not on the jetty.'

'Is it seaworthy?'

'It looks all right.'

She gave a deprecating laugh. 'Oh, it *looks* all right. Suppose it's not? Suppose it sinks?'

'I didn't have long to check it over, did I? How long was I gone before I told the boatman we didn't need the return ride? Ten minutes?'

Linda was on her feet. 'I want to see the boat for myself.'

With a lazy movement he splashed more whisky into their glasses. 'It's too dark now. I'll show you in the morning.'

'Now, Tom. Before daylight goes completely.'

'Leave it. We're here for the night anyway.'

She went to the window and pressed her face close to the glass. He was right, it was too late. In a minute she went and sat down again, joining him in the wavering circle of yellow lamplight. He began to tell her stories about the people who had stayed in this house when he and his family were in the one that was scarcely better than a shed. Linda did not bother to work out where the boundary between fact and fiction might be. After all, some of the strangest things turned out to be true so what did it matter?

Unbidden, the lines of the Herrick poem came into her head.

Here we are all day by day; by night we're hurled
By dreams, each one, into a several world.

She thought: '*He got it wrong. We live in separate worlds in our waking lives too. How simple it would be if the differences existed only while we slept.*'

9

Pacing her cell, the woman counted her steps. Six from the window to the door. Eight from the rock wall to the one with the pegs. Ten if she crossed the room diagonally. Twenty-eight if she walked around the perimeter. But sometimes the figures were different. Either she lost count or, when she took the other diagonal, she counted nine and not ten. It was a while before she understood why the two diagonals were not identical. The rock wall was not straight, that was the answer. When she realised, she was annoyed to have been puzzled because the explanation was obvious.

To keep her mind active she turned to mathematics. Other captives had done that and swore it had helped, so she embarked on a series of useless calculations. How long were her steps, how long and how wide was the room, how high? How many square feet or yards or metres? What was the cubic measurement? Then she attempted to correlate the speed of the tide creeping up a rock to the hands of a clock moving round the face. Designed as a challenge to her concentration, it became baroque. Smaller calculations clustered around the main one. Instead of one mathematical endeavour she was grappling with half a dozen. The wind, for instance, seemed to have a bearing on the speed of the water's creeping and she tried to assess that before she returned to the central question.

Eventually she accepted it was beyond her and, dispirited and weary, gave up. She had never been especially proficient at mathematics anyway and mental arithmetic of such complexity was over ambitious. Later, she thought, she might try simpler sums, just to prove to herself that she was not completely incapable.

Outside the sea tantalised her with its coming and going. Driftwood floated by on the current. The silvery wings of a faraway aeroplane caught the sun as it flew over the islands. She felt light, as though she too might float or fly, if she were free to go.

117

Soon after the hornet buzz of the aeroplane had died, something else winked in the sun. A car windscreen, she guessed. There were no houses on that stretch of the main island and she believed the road ran to the east, but perhaps there was a track to a hidden house or up into the mountains.

She felt a rush of excitement before she had articulated the thought: if a car driver could accidentally signal to her then she could signal back. And she had the means, she had a tin.

Scrabbling across the floor she snatched the tin from the shelf and practised at the window, easing herself into the recess and stretching her arm through the bars. She was in shadow, she would have to wait until the sun arced round, but then, she was sure, she could do it.

She flopped on to the floor and hugged the tin. Everything was going to be all right after all, she actually dared to believe it. With an ironic smile she thought that all she had to do was wait a few hours, and that was no problem, she was used to waiting. The nonsense about attaching a message to a gull embarrassed her now that the simple, sensible solution had been thought of. Once again it astonished her how slowly she was thinking because this ought to have occurred to her days ago. But she preferred to enjoy the relief of finding her way out rather than to lament her stupidity.

Another sum needed to be done, a calculation about the length of time before the sun reached her window. There was purpose in this, it focused her mind on something positive and practical. Of course, it made no difference whether she got the answer right or wrong because she would be there waiting whenever the sun arrived, but she wanted to work it out anyway.

While she was struggling with the calculation, she examined the tin closely. Previously it had been a tool to gouge a plaster ceiling, or a chunk of metal to clang against the door and create maximum noise. Now she considered it purely as a reflector. It would benefit from polishing, she decided.

With spit and one of her tissues she cleaned it up and then she sat buffing it on the sleeve of her jacket, wishing she could think of a more effective way. The repetitive action soothed her, encouraging her thoughts to meander while she sat there, by her window, eyes on the other shore. Every so often she stopped polishing, raised the tin and angled it to catch the light. She was willing to believe it was getting shinier.

She imagined herself a princess in a fairytale, polishing a gold ring so that she could signal her distress to a passing knight. Fairy-tales had happy endings for the good and come-uppances for the bad, they were comforting. Her personal version had a peculiarly Celtic flavour because her saviour would come across the water. In Celtic legends they often did. While her estranged husband had been interpreting the tumbled stones of Welsh and Irish history she had been dreamily remembering the stories. There was a beauty in them that charmed her. She thought of Bran who taught a starling to speak and sent it across the Irish Sea to plead for her rescue; of white flowers that sprang from the earth wherever Olwen left a footprint; of Blodeuwedd whose punishment was to be transformed into an owl made of flowers.

Blodeuwedd's fate set her brooding on her own folly and the punishment she was suffering. She had set out to deceive and had fallen in with a greater deceiver. Nothing that happened had been spontaneous, he had steered a course. She wondered how long he had been trailing around the wintry countryside looking for a woman like her, one who thought herself independent but could be bent to his will.

If his eyes were not windows to his mind, perhaps his stories were. She sifted them for clues but found only a recurrent theme: the powerlessness of children. The stories of her own childhood were comfortable in comparison. Even the saga of the teapots, which had infuriated her while she was living through it, seemed no worse than quirky. Presumably, she thought, the fault lay in her telling of it. People always sniggered, because she failed to convey the threat, the crowding in, the crushing of her young spirit. The poet in her recognised it as a metaphor for mother-daughter conflict in a house where they were the only two. The pity of it was that her mother had won each round. Not, apart from that one screaming match, by fierce confrontation but by barging ahead in a very kindly fashion.

Little wonder, she thought, that she had grown up to be a dis-carder, a chucker-out, a clearer of cupboards, a creature who cringed at words like collector. Working in the bookshop she had learned not to wince when Jerome talked deferentially about the collectors he had met. She tried to share his enthusiasm for a future as a dealer in old and rare books, and she quelled her misgivings when, going upstairs to his flat, she noticed how the extra stock kept needing extra shelves and the passageway and bathroom were being overtaken. It was all terribly, depressingly familiar.

A bird wailed, close by the window. She watched it flick aside, out of her view. Then she checked the shine on the tin, looking for her face on its surface like a fairytale heroine seeking a way out of her tower. But this was tin and not mirror, and the vague patch of colour did not count as a face. She lay the tin down by the window where it would be ready for the sun. Then she stood up and walked towards the door.

The door leaned in on her, the walls pressed forward. Six steps, eight steps, nine or ten steps. She knew what the measurements should be but the cellar was shrinking and the figures were wrong. Thrusting out her hands she tried to push the walls out, to make them stand upright and not fall and crush her. Worst was the rock that bellied into the room because this was growing, a great black hump consuming her space. With a howl she staggered back, touched the wall which had the row of nails sticking out of it and she pushed against it, her eyes shut.

When next she looked the room was its usual shape, the distortion had finished. One white wall was freckled with sunlight from the sea. She half ran, half fell towards the window and seized the tin. Soon, very soon, it would be time. Tense, eager and determined, she waited.

Way out on the water a dull patch was floating. Twisting her head, she looked up at the cloud. Others were leaving the mountains where they had hung around all day. A scene that had been bright for hours was becoming mottled with shadow. It was going to be a gamble whether the sun was visible when it passed across her window. The minutes slid by, the clouds merged and broke away, the sun was brilliant and then absent. Over and over, the scene outside her window was shifting.

The mountains had become a hazy bulk. She worried that a mist on the big island would prevent her signal being seen. Then the mountains were gone altogether, there was only a shoreline and low hills. A streaky sky told her it was raining on the higher land.

But on the sound the sun was forcing its way through cloud every few minutes, unwilling to give up, just as though it was on her side. And when it came to it, the sun reached down and lit the beach and she crammed herself into the recess and stuck her arm right out through the bars. Her skin changed colour as it moved from the pallid light of the cellar and into the pure light of day, but there was no gold in the fine hairs of her arm because she could not reach from shadow into sun. Waggling the tin about, she prayed that it was flashing. There was no way of being sure.

The cloud came and went and the sun wandered on. She sank back on the floor, her arms painful where she had been stretching and straining. What might it have looked like from the other side of the water, she wondered? An urgent bid for rescue or just another sparkle among a sea of sparkling waves? A tower would have been better, her cell was too close to the sea.

The mountains remained screened by rain, and the sky above the sound became unbroken cloud. The sea grew rougher and the gulls relinquished their favourite perch on the rocks and flew inland. A boat appeared, from the direction of the harbour. Her heart gave a great leap of joy but she was too terrified of disappointment to take chances. Immediately, she had the tin out of the window again and was waving it about and shouting. Her first signal and now the first boat, it was surely too pat to be coincidence. She kept on flashing the tin, hoping that despite the lack of sun she might catch someone's eye. And this time she was sure there was someone out there who would be looking.

She pictured the crew, someone busy with fishing gear, someone else keeping an eye on the worsening weather. Say they had seen her signal and were coming to check it out before going on to the fishing grounds, then they would turn the boat towards her any minute. But say it was coincidence, that they had not seen her flashes and were simply off on a fishing trip, then the man whose job it was to watch the weather would be staring all around and was bound to look her way. With all the energy she could summon she waved the tin.

The boat did not veer towards her. It sailed away down the sound.

10

Tom slept heavily after drinking all that whisky but his snoring woke Linda not long after daybreak. She was cold. For a few minutes she lay quietly, watching the weak light through the window growing brighter and listening for the beat of the surf on the shore. The snoring made that difficult but instead of shutting Tom up, by nudging him until he turned on his side, she decided to get dressed.

She gathered up her clothes and tiptoed out of the room into the kitchen, steadying the door to prevent it crashing back or screeching on its hinges. It had made an alarming noise the evening before.

The kitchen was no warmer than the bedroom. She hankered again for a peat fire. If they had lit one when she suggested it the kitchen would have been a pool of warmth now. She switched on the radio to take her mind off the cold but all she heard was a hissing, a pathetic diminuendo that died away in seconds. Quickly she dragged on her clothes, took her jacket from the back of one of the kitchen chairs and put that on too. Washing was impossible, the water was not turned on. Tom had mentioned a tap outside but neither of them had gone round in the dark to find it.

Linda opened the door on to a crisp morning that promised to grow sunny. The sky to the east was streaked with gold. Several mornings had started this way, with thin clear colours beneath a pale and slightly cloudy sky. Then the sun had washed over the scene.

Seeking the tap, she went round to the back of the house. There was no problem about finding it now that it was light. It was fixed to the wall, where she judged the kitchen to be. A black plastic hose was connected to it. She wondered whether the supply came from a spring or whether it was taken from the stream she and Tom had leaped across. Although she struggled with the tap, it was too stiff for her to turn it. Disappointed, she began to follow the pipe, which lay like a plump licorice bootlace draped alongside a track on the hillside.

After a while the pipe veered away and shot up through a crevice between some rocks. But by then Linda had been distracted from it. At each step her view opened up further, until she could see a dozen islands floating on the water; cloud hooked on the soaring mountains of the main island; a dainty-footed sheep nibbling near the waterline.

Spotting the roof of the simple house where Tom spent his youthful holidays, she made her way over to it. She had not liked to think of this when they were there together but it was going to collapse before long. A wall was bowed. Nobody would patch the roof and once a roof was gone a building was finished. Tom saw the house as it used to be, his eyes refused to see anything else, but viewed calmly in the morning light, without his stories to tailor her imagination, all she saw was a derelict house about to become tumbledown.

'Good thing he got here in time,' she thought. 'He'd have been heartbroken if he'd come and found a pile of stones.'

She was about to move away when a chilly wind stirred and she automatically stepped inside to shelter from it. Her eye went to the black streak that ran from the hearth to the chimney. She touched it, but it was not the thick fluffy soot she had supposed. There had not been a fire for years. What was left was a stain.

A heap of rubble was gathering in the corner below the damaged roof. She foresaw the decline, the dilapidation: more of the roof would fall in, a roof support would give way, the bowing wall would topple. Probably the doorway might survive longest, they frequently did, but it would stand as a doorway to nothing. This day it was still a doorway to memories, to dreams.

Sheep droppings littered the floor but they were old and crumbling to dust. The animals had not bothered with the place for some time. Grass that they had once reshaped with their teeth was growing again, the blades squared off. Only the new shoots were tapered and undamaged.

Linda went outside and sat on a rock with her back against the rough stone wall. To the east the sky and the sea burned with flames of gold, the snow on the highest peaks was alight with it. She thought of rushing down and rousing Tom, to share with him this most exquisite morning. Then she wanted it all for herself instead. He had his own memories of the island, plenty of them, plain or exaggerated.

'*This one will be mine,*' she thought. '*In the little time that's left to me, before he wakes up and we launch the boat and go away from here for ever, I want to enjoy this on my own.*'

A phrase came to her. She felt in her pocket for a pen and a piece of paper. Her fingers touched newsprint. Linda drew it out and unfolded the pages. She looked again at the image of Anita Gayner.

It struck her that the woman seemed familiar. Anita was wearing an evening dress and her hair was hooked up at one side with a ribbon. She had been photographed at a gathering: pieces of other people's bodies and garments encroached on the picture. Anita was smiling, self consciously, as if to say she did not choose to be photographed but was making the best of it. If she were at a dinner and a photographer was doing the rounds of the tables, snapping at diners without their say-so, then this was quite likely the smile she would smile.

'*And yet,*' Linda thought, '*I do know her. Is it possible I'm remembering the publicity from two years ago when she went off?*'

She decided that was not the answer. Anita Gayner's disappearance had been a local issue, not a national one. Strathblane was disturbed but hardly London. Anita was not a vulnerable teenager, she was twenty-eight, single and free to do as she liked. If she had wearied of her life and abandoned it for a fresh one, then she was doing no more than countless women dreamed of doing every day. The difference was that she had gone and she had been found dead. Two years later. Close to home. Linda wondered whether Anita did not look like an actress, a female politician, someone she 'knew' in the way one knows famous faces on television. She tried out several names but, although they had features in common with Anita, none of them truly resembled her.

She analysed the image. Anita was overweight, or at any rate the photographer had not flattered her because there was the hint of a double chin and her arms, sticking out of the sleeveless evening dress, were thick and fleshy. If she had been younger Anita could have blamed puppy fat.

Linda concentrated on the face, imagining how it would be altered if the hair hung loosely around it. With her fingers she covered the ears. Then she cramped her hand around the face, pretending a fringe and a short hair cut. The eyes gazed up at her and she realised then that it was the set of the eyes and the lift of the eyebrows that she had been striving to match. They were not like the eyes of the actresses or the models or the other wellknown women she had called to mind. And yet she knew them.

She saw too that it was the mouth and the way the head was held that prevented the smile being whole-hearted. The eyes were untroubled, and she knew them.

She switched her attention away from the photograph and read the words again. This slow second reading revealed something she had missed before. The wording was curious. The journalist, and the police and fire service spokesmen who were quoted, appeared to be skirting around something. What was it Mrs Macmuddle had said: *'There's something we're not being told.'* Linda believed her after all.

The nub of it was that no one was coming straight out and saying the woman had been killed in the fire. There was talk of the body being discovered in the part of the castle that burned; and the body was said to have been identified by the teeth, which matched the dental chart of the missing Anita Gayner, but no one actually said the woman died in the fire. And if she had not, then how had she died?

Linda refolded the paper, pressed it as flat as it would go and put it back in her inside pocket. As soon as they got over to the main island she would buy a paper and see whether all was revealed in the follow up story. There was bound to be one, the story would not be dropped until as much of the mystery was revealed as possible.

She got up from her rock and headed for the other house. Hunger was niggling at her. Their supper had been scant, just bread and the contents of a couple of the tins Tom had brought, plus far too much whisky. In the cupboard was a jar of instant coffee, she had noted that and planned to steal enough for a couple of cups once the water was turned on. The prospect was wonderful: a cup of instant coffee and a hunk of the leftover bread, and she would be happy to jump on the boat with him and wait for a proper breakfast. Oatcakes? Porridge? Sausages? Yes, everything that was on offer, she would eat.

Tom was in the kitchen. He had turned the water on and was gouging the contents of the coffee jar with a knife.

'Concrete,' he said.

'Damn, I was relying on that stuff.'

She took her jacket off and hung it over the back of a wooden kitchen chair. Then she opened the cupboard door and scanned the shelves, seeking alternatives.

He said: 'There's no tea, I've checked.'

She shrugged: 'Oh, well, fresh spring water, then. I'm sure it's healthier anyway.'

The glasses were smeared with whisky. She held them under running water in the sink until they shone clean, then filled a glass and drank.

Tom said: 'That ought to be filtered, you know.'

She looked at him stupidly, not sure whether this was a joke. In cities you filtered water to rid it of things the water authorities had added. Who was adding anything to a natural supply like this?

'Sheep,' Tom said. 'They might have fouled the stream. What you've got in that glass comes from the stream. The pipe's wedged into it high up.'

She hesitated, the glass half full, her thirst half quenched. 'Oh, I expect it's all right. It can't do much harm, can it?'

'What if a sheep fell in it and died there? Have you walked the length of the stream to check it?'

'No.'

'I'm going to do that next.'

This seemed pointless as they were soon to leave, but she assumed he meant he wanted the walk. Rather than hurry him to get back to the main island, she said: 'All right, we'll go together.'

He handed her the jacket. She imagined or heard the newspaper crackling in the pocket, she did not know which.

The licorice bootlace went up through a cleft in some rocks and met the stream a hundred yards on. They clambered on up, all the way to the source of the stream. No dead sheep, nothing worrying or questionable. Tom hooked out some overhanging weeds and then declared their water supply as good as could be expected. He scooped a mouthful in his hand and shivered for the coldness of it.

'The boat,' Linda said. 'That's next.'

So they went to the boat. This lay dragged up into a cove well above the tideline. It was a cheap fibreglass affair, tipped over on a patch of land that had not settled whether to be grass or sand. The boat seemed sound enough, there were no gaping holes or suspicious dents.

Tom said: 'The tide's wrong, we'll have to wait for it.'

The delay did not upset her. He was obviously right and the important thing was that the boat looked seaworthy. Until the tide came and they were able to launch it, appearances were all they had to go on.

He said: 'The motor's in the cellar up at the house. I'll get that fixed up and then we'll be ready to go when there's some water.'

Instead of returning immediately to the house, he strolled down to the rocks. Linda followed, silently cursing the MacTwaddles for preferring not to keep their boat on the jetty. The purpose of a jetty was to allow boats to come and go when the owners wanted, so why have a jetty and not use it?

Tom picked up her thoughts. 'If it's left bouncing around on the jetty, the winter storms will smash it to pulp. They've done the wise thing, pulling it up into a protected area.'

'But how did they get away if this is their boat?'

That turned out to be another wise thing they had done: hiring a boat to take them across and leaving their own runabout where it was safe from thieves and meddlers.

The tops of the rocks were greasy with lichen but lower down crustacea clung, the usual limpets, whelks and mussels, each shell an arrangement of delicate whorls. Tiny round holes marred several of the shells.

'Tom, why aren't we hiring a boat too? If we take this one over there, then over there it will have to stay. Besides, if people see us with this boat they'll wonder why we're using it.'

He was ready for that. 'The guy who brought us out believes I'm a MacTwaddle.'

'You pretended to be one of the family?'

'He wasn't going to contradict me, was he?'

She felt uneasy and wished he had not told her, but he thought it was funny and rather clever. Linda bit her lip and hoped there would be no more disconcerting revelations before the tide turned.

She asked him instead about the holed shells. 'It can't be a bird damaging them, can it?'

Tom pointed to a couple of shells that were stuck together, one mounted on the other. 'That's what does it.'

Fleetingly she thought the pair were copulating but Tom said: 'The dog whelk is a predator. It attaches itself to a shell, bores a hole through and devours its captive.' He reached down and tapped the shells with his foot before adding: 'It's almost mauve, that means its meal is nearly finished.' Then he glanced at Linda to check she was attending. 'Did you know the monks used to write with the purple ink it secretes? Or that the Romans used it to dye their togas?'

She laughed. 'What is this? Quiz night at the local pub?'

127

'Can I have another point for saying the dye's called purpurin?'

'No, you lose three for showing off.'

'I'd better shut up, then.'

But they joked about it all the way back to the house. He said he had learned it all from a book when he was a child, and it was grisly enough to have stuck in his mind. No doubt, he said, there was plenty of dull stuff about seaweed in the same volume but that hadn't the same excitement and he had forgotten it.

Cautious after his warning, Linda boiled water and let it cool before she drank any more of it. While it was cooling she spread a hunk of bread with pate from another of the tins. She sat at the kitchen table and ate her breakfast. Tom was outside, examining the engine.

After eating she went down to the cellar. She had noticed it from outside, the barred window where the house became two storeys instead of one.

'Be careful if you go in there,' Tom said. 'The door can slam.'

In fact he had jacked it open, as she saw once she was half way down the steps to it. These steps led off a lobby that opened into the kitchen. Directly above the cellar was the bedroom. It crossed her mind that it would be possible to open the wrong door in the kitchen and pitch down the steps by accident.

The room was bare and square, the door solid and the window lacked glass. It was a peculiar room in a peculiar house. She was puzzled why the house had evolved this way and why no one troubled to change the rooms around. Then, having seen the little there was to see in the cellar, she ran upstairs and closed the lobby door on it.

Midway between the lobby and the kitchen table, realisation hit her with the force of a blow. Anita Gayner was not a face on a television screen, she was a face in a photograph album. Tom's album.

A hand cupped her mouth, and her legs crumpled. Linda grabbed the back of a chair to support herself.

'Ridiculous, you can't be right!' Yet even as she argued against it she knew she was.

The wad of paper in her pocket was pressing against her heart, and her heart was lurching. If he put his head into the kitchen he would see her flushed and shocked.

'Whatever happens, he mustn't know.' She forced her legs to be strong, to get her as far as the sink and a glass of reviving water.

Her own words, recalled from days ago, were taunting her. *'Number eight. Perhaps I'm number eight.'*

Linda gulped down the water and shot a glance at the door. Tom was some way off, carrying the engine to the boat. That would take time, that *gave* her time.

Recovering her strength, she rushed to the bedroom and grabbed his bag. Kneeling beside it she rummaged through clothes, found bank notes a-plenty but could not lay her hands on the album. It had to be there, it had always been there, where else might he have put it? Could he have left it in the hire car? No reason for him to do that. No, it must be here somewhere. She calmed herself and tried again, searching more thoroughly. Nothing.

Once she broke off, thinking she heard him approaching the house. Sauntering through to the kitchen, desperate to look unruffled, she checked. No Tom. Then a splutter of engine noise from the direction of the cove convinced her he was nowhere near. She dashed back to the bedroom and the bag.

At last she came upon the album, in a side pocket. Afraid, now that she had proof in her hand, she dithered, lacking the courage to open it and know the truth. Then, spurred by the same fear, she turned the pages.

Number one was fair with permed hair. Two had big hair and big shoulder pads. Three was the youngest, the one with leggings and untidy hair. Four was an elfin blonde in denims. Five was plump with mousey bobbed hair. Six was Anita Gayner.

Linda checked the door again, racing on tiptoe. She heard no engine noise this time but neither did she see Tom. Then she was kneeling once more, dragging the newspaper cutting from her pocket and comparing. The eyes, the eyebrows. Yes, she had been right. The woman was Anita Gayner, or if not she was remarkably like her. There would always, of course, be room for that doubt.

With unwelcome clarity she understood how Tom had always existed for her amidst doubts. That was the excitement of knowing him, that was the charm and the adventure. Was he this or that? Had he done this or that? And now, what might he do next?

He called her.

She gave a start, stuffed the album into the bag and the newspaper into her pocket, anyhow, no longer neatly folded, no longer flat and unobtrusive. He would notice, he could not fail to. Her wild imagination convinced her the line of her jacket was distorted by the bulk, that the paper was uncrumpling inside the pocket, forcing the jacket more and more out of shape, until she seemed to be wearing a lopsidedly inflated lifejacket.

And before she could remedy it, Tom came in.

'Oh, there you are. I was calling you. Didn't you hear?'

'I . . .'

She felt his attention riveted by the out of shape jacket, his gaze penetrating the cloth, his eyes reading the newsprint.

He said: 'Are you OK? You look a bit . . .'

'A headache.' She put a hand to her brow in silly theatrical demonstration of a headache. Then her legs grew unreliable again and she sat down heavily on the edge of the bed.

'Oh, God,' she thought. *'Now he's going to sit down too and ask if there's anything he can do for me, and he'll see the mess I've made of the bag as well as seeing my puffed up pocket and then . . . Oh, God.'*

To her amazement she heard: 'You'll be all right to come on the boat, won't you?'

He stayed where he was, a couple of steps into the room.

She nodded anxiously. 'Yes, I'll be fine. I'll take some painkillers.'

Even if her legs let her down and she had to drag herself on her knees to the boat, she was not going to miss that tide. Every moment she remained on the island was torture. Once across the water everything would be different. There were people there. She would have options and opportunities. She would do what her instinct had begged her to do days ago, she would get away from him. But first she must cross that span of water.

Tom said: 'You could lie down for an hour. We're not in any hurry.'

Linda cleared her throat and asked, in as firm a voice as she could muster, whether he would mind bringing her a glass of water to wash down the pills.

When he had gone she fetched the pills from her sponge bag and, while crouching by her own bag, straightened his so that it looked less disordered. But there was nothing she could do about the turmoil inside her. Her brain was reeling with rash ideas for escape. Nonsense, they were all nonsense and she bullied herself to reject them. The only wise course was to do nothing, to let time pass until the tide was ready to carry her to safety.

Tom returned with a tumbler of water. She was already lying down, the pills in her hand. She murmured thanks and swallowed them. He said he was going down to the boat but would look in shortly and see how she was. Linda lay back and closed her eyes.

He reached the bedroom doorway before saying: 'You can get under the quilt, if you like. You don't need that thick jacket on in here. Let me help you take it off.'

Unable to prevent him doing so, she mumbled thanks. Then she watched him carry the jacket out into the kitchen.

'*Number eight.*' The words beat a rhythm in her skull, and the headache she had feigned became real.

Time passed sluggishly. Several times she threw off the quilt and went to the window to check the level of the tide but its progress was imperceptible. It had covered several more inches of a particular rock between her peeps but she had forgotten which mark on the rock was her reference point. Anxiety was making her inefficient.

The surf ought to have lulled her but she was measuring its level: the louder it was, the nearer. Rest was out of the question. Eventually she gave up and went into the kitchen. Tom was there, seated by the table. She had heard no noises from indoors and taken it to mean he was fussing over the boat or else prowling around his island.

An expression of amusement danced across his face as she flinched. 'I made you jump?'

'You've been so quiet, I didn't know you were here.'

She was relieved to hear herself sounding no more rattled than anyone surprised under normal circumstances. But the relief was very shortlived because on the table was spread the newspaper she had crammed in her pocket. Tom had made an effort to smooth it out but it lay there, bumpy like a model of a contour map. Anita Gayner's face was warped.

He said: 'You were rustling.'

Her jaw tightened, defiant. She did not answer.

Tom said: 'It's not like you to steal something from a bar. You must have been especially interested in it.'

She shrugged but it was impossible to bring off the nonchalant gesture she required. The result looked as though she was jerking away from him, or from dealing with an unpalatable truth.

Tom stuck out a foot and pushed the other kitchen chair away from the table, indicating she was to sit down. Linda turned to the door instead, saying she felt like some air.

He said: 'It's cold out there.'

And as she opened the door a breeze flew across the room and lifted the paper into the air. Tom slammed it down on to the table with his palm. The noise and the rapid movements coupled with the rush of cold frightened Linda. Although she needed to run, anywhere, she was rooted.

Then Tom was at her side, drawing her in and closing the door. He was gentle with her but in control again.

She struggled to speak normally. 'How much longer until we can get the boat out?'

'About half an hour.' His strong hands were flattening Anita Gayner's face. Her evening dress grew svelte under his caress and her eyes smiled up at him.

Linda stemmed a shudder. He was indifferent, she thought, and that was unnatural. The woman's body had been found in the castle where they had spent a night, and he was utterly untroubled.

'We must tidy up,' she said, glad she had thought of something practical to occupy the half hour that was left to her. 'We can't leave this mess for the MacTwaddles when they come out next.'

She stuffed things back into cupboards and drawers, hastily, wishing her hands were not betraying her by trembling. As she ran water into the sink for washing up, she heard the scrape of chair legs on the stone floor and then she felt Tom watching her. To distract him, she coerced him into helping.

'I left a glass in the bedroom, Tom.'

There was no reply but she heard him walk down the room. Linda leaned over the edge of the sink, her hands clasped tight together beneath the foam of the washing up liquid.

'Let me get through this,' she prayed. *'Half an hour, that's all I ask. Let me hold out for half an hour.'*

Then, hearing his returning footsteps, she deliberately relaxed and began to wash up the breakfast dishes. Tom put the tumbler down on the draining board, ready for her.

'Thank you.'

He probably missed her quiet words as he was immediately on his way to the bedroom again. She risked a backward glance and was in time to catch sight of his sleeve as he disappeared into the other room. She dried the crockery.

As she wiped each item she gazed out of the window, noticing where the surf was drawing its white line. The rocks Tom had fished from as a boy were almost all covered except for the craggier ones. Gulls played around them, like paddling children dodging breakers.

She put the plates and glasses away in the cupboard and returned the bottle of washing up liquid to the shelf behind the curtain below the sink. Then she looked all around, eager for something else to do. There was only her packing but she preferred not to go into the bedroom while he was there.

Linda folded the newspaper, wanting it flat and neat and hidden, as though it mattered any more. Before she had finished, Tom called her.

His bag was on one of the beds. For a second she assumed he was going to complain that she had been nosing through it, but instead he urged her to hurry up with her own packing.

'Yes, sorry, I was tidying up out there.' She thrust a few scattered bits and pieces into her bag and announced it was ready to go. Then she puffed up pillows and straightened the quilt. There was nothing more to be done about the bed, except hope that the MacTwaddles did not learn they had given refuge to uninvited guests.

While she was patting and smoothing, Tom said he was going down to the boat. She was surprised, when she finished with the bed, to notice her bag on the floor where it had been all along. He had taken only his own.

Just then the front door swung, a blast of cold air swirled through the house and the door banged. Linda hoisted her bag, ready to run after him. But as she lifted it clear of the floor she discovered it had been resting on a green plastic folder, the photograph album. She felt a pang of horror. This was the very last thing she would have chosen to find. She dared not hand the album to him because she did not want to discuss it. Far from it, she hoped he would never realise she knew of its existence. Two possibilities occurred to her. Either she must hide it in the bedroom or else she must put it in her own bag and transfer it to his later.

With shaking hands she knelt and put it in, on top of her sponge bag and alongside the notebook where she was writing her new poem.

Linda helped Tom launch the boat. They turned it over and then half-dragged and half-lifted it a few yards down the sandy, grassy cove until it reached the water. Then they paddled in, holding it steady so that it kept upright and was not flooded. Although the sea was calm, for every few waves that wasted themselves idly on the shore there was one that smashed in fury. Tom watched the breakers coming in and judged the exact moment to surrender the boat to the water, safely.

Then he sprang aboard, making the boat bounce and surge

through the spray until he could coax her along with an oar towards the jetty. Almost at once one of the bigger waves caught her and spun her, threatening to send her sideways back where she had come from. His oar became a pole, pushing her off, jiggling her round, outwitting the eager waves.

It was Linda's job to walk round to the jetty once the boat was afloat and be ready to hand over their bags which they had left there. When Tom jumped on board she stumbled out of the surf, with great splashing footsteps, and watched his manoeuvres. A gull cut between them and drifted down to perch on her bag. She set off for the jetty, thankful to be on the point of departure but sad too. The place was beautiful, peaceful, all the things she had thought she wanted. Under other circumstances she would have begged to stay on, but this situation was appalling: she was with a man who was a frightening stranger and she had convicted him of murder.

Yes, now that she was within minutes of escaping from him she allowed the word. Murder.

Sharp with herself, she put an end to that line of thought. *Stop dramatising!* It was enough that she was about to leave him, she need not get upset at this stage. She had managed to endure the hours waiting for the tide, the tough part was over, all she had to do was keep calm and unquestioning and avoid potentially dangerous subjects. In a minute he would have the boat alongside the jetty, she would pass him the bags and step aboard. Then he would start up the engine, fouling the air with diesel, and without lingering they would head across the sound to a safe harbour. She liked the ring of that: safe harbour.

Tom brought the boat to the jetty. She lifted one of the bags but at the same instant he tossed her a rope and she dropped the bag and held the rope instead. He scrambled on to the jetty.

'We tie up to this,' he said, and looped the rope around a jagged stone that stood taller than the rest.

Until then she had seen it purely as a popular perch for the gulls. Now that Tom had pointed out its purpose, it was obvious. Linda moved the bags to the edge, stepped down into the boat and lifted them in. She placed them carefully, so that their weight was equally distributed and the craft would not tilt. Then, moving delicately, she went to the prow and sat on the wooden slat that made a seat. All the time the boat was quivering, a movement she hated. It made her feel insubstantial, underlining that she had to risk her very life to elements beyond her control. Her hand clutched the rough grey stone beside her but that did not help. She rose and fell beside her stationary hand, she was pulled away from it and pushed up to it, through her whole body she could feel the tug of the tide.

She thought of climbing ashore until the engine was started but she chewed her lower lip and determined to sit it out. To risk delay was madness, and Tom was already dithering. After securing the rope he had stayed on the jetty.

Linda teased him. 'Come on, you've had your treat. It's all over now.'

He squatted to speak to her. 'We could stay, you know. It's not like it used to be, dashing off to be in time for the first day of school.'

'Are you serious?'

The question was out before she had marshalled the words in her head. She was being ironically disbelieving, but although the words were right the question was ambiguous. Unfortunately, it was also what one said if one hoped an offer was genuine.

'Yes,' he said, very matter of fact. 'I don't know why we ever thought of going today.'

Linda made no move to get out of the boat. She fought down her fierce resistance to the idea of staying and said, in a way that suggested she had been weighing up the disadvantages: 'Well, the first reason is that there's next to no food here.'

'There are several tins in that cupboard.'

As if in reply her stomach rumbled its emptiness. He did not notice and she said: 'I had tins yesterday and I'm starving. We're out of bread now and the only thing we have to drink apart from water from the stream is whisky.'

He pulled a face. 'But we could manage.'

She shook her head. 'We did that last night and this morning. This island needs more food, Tom.'

He laughed, standing up, freeing the damp trouser legs where they clung to his skin. 'We could always kill a sheep, I suppose.'

'Or you could clamber out on the rocks and fish for a shark.' She jabbed a finger at the other seat in the boat. 'Come on, let's be on our way.'

But he was staring up at the hill, in the direction of the near ruin where he had once spent his holidays.

'Tom.' She paused until he turned his head. Afraid that he was scheming to walk up there again and make trouble about them leaving, she had thought of a ploy.

'Listen, Tom. Why don't we go shopping for food and come back?'

His face lit up. She hurried on, adding fresh ideas as she went.

'Yes,' she said. 'We could round up some more groceries, and get a new battery for that old radio, and we could buy a torch too, so that we won't be carrying a teetering oil lamp from room to room once night falls.'

Catching what he took to be her enthusiasm, he added a few items to the list, matches in particular.

Linda was making it sound so attractive, she almost believed in it herself. *'Perhaps you have to,'* she thought, *'to be a convincing liar.'* What she intended to do was escape once the boat reached harbour. Safe harbour. He could buy whatever provisions he liked, but nothing on earth would persuade her to return to the island.

Tom said: 'Great. Well, in that case there's no rush, is there? If we're only going there and back we needn't set off for ages.'

He bent and held out a hand to help her up from the boat. Linda's fingers kept their grip on the slat she was sitting on.

'But the tide,' she said. 'We've waited so long for this.'

'Only because the boat was in the cove. There isn't a problem now, we can take off from the jetty whenever it suits us.'

He was scoffing at her for being muddled, and she was filled with despair and torn apart by the necessity of concealing it. She averted her face. Waves were licking the jetty, shimmering on the spread of water and, far off, riding the water like a flock of swans. Buildings on the main island were a broken chain of pale rectangles. The harbour itself was concealed behind a headland. Linda swallowed hard and failed to think of a fresh argument.

'Tom, I want to go now.'

She was looking up at him, speaking in a plain way that brooked no misunderstanding and made her sound unpersuadable.

'I don't.' His tone matched her own.

This was worse than she had feared. Until that bald statement she had hoped he would be brought round by argument or, if that failed, by what amounted to an appeal to respect her wishes. But he was implacable. He stared at her for a moment more and then walked away across the beach.

Linda let out a huge sigh, a muted groan. She felt she had mis-handled the situation, although it was not obvious what she ought to have done instead. She had obeyed her instinct to avoid outright confrontation but they had ended up with a veiled one. And it came to the same thing: Tom was in charge and would do nothing except what he chose to do.

Her hand dragged against the grey stone wall. The tide teased her, luring her out into the sound.

'I could go,' she thought. *'Let him stay here on his own, that's what he wants. I could tweak the rope from around the stone, and let the boat drift for the first yard or two. Then I'll start the engine – and I'm away!'*

It was the bit about the engine that daunted her. Suppose it did not start because of her incompetence? She had never used one. Suppose she drifted out into the sound? Or on to rocks?

'You're creating problems that don't exist,' she objected. *'A two stroke engine, that's what it is. You've used one on a mower. It can't be much different.'*

Without leaving her seat she studied what she could see of the engine that Tom had fixed to the stern before launching the boat. He had tested it and confirmed it was in working order, she had heard the familiar rasping noise. There was a knob and she deduced that one twisted or pulled that to get the thing going.

Linda made up her mind. Careful not to tip the boat, she stood up and reached for the rope that secured it to the jetty. She gave a sharp tug. Her hand smarted as it skimmed down the rope. The rope itself did not shift, except to tighten around the rock. To free it, she was going to have to get out.

Unused to boats, she could not think how to organise all this. What bothered her was the business of boarding once she had unhooked the rope. If she, on the jetty and holding the rope in her hands, was all that was keeping the boat snug against the wall, then how was she to get aboard? Surely as soon as she slackened her pull on the rope, the boat would be carried away and she would be faced with a chasm to jump across. How did people do it?

While she was trying to work it out, Tom came striding over the beach. The moment was lost. As it happened, he misinterpreted what he saw.

'Don't worry,' he called over. 'I'll give you a hand with those.'

'Oh, thanks.' She had no clue what he was talking about and was simply relieved that he sounded unperturbed.

Tom crouched and lifted out their bags. 'We can leave them here, they'll be safe enough. But you were right to think they shouldn't stay on board. You never know, they could get drenched or even tipped out if someone comes charging by in a power boat.'

137

With an easy lie she said that was what had been concerning her. She despised herself for the lie and for her acquiescence, but the damage was done. It had been done weeks ago when she had let him into her life and allowed him to rearrange it. To begin with it had seemed harmless, rather entertaining, and by the time she had realised how manipulative he was, it had been too late to do anything about it except leave him. For the previous few days she had not even had that chance. All this went round and round in her head while Tom was dumping the bags on the jetty and leading her inland.

They climbed again to the pinnacle rock and she contrived a few quips as she had done the first time. They prowled along paths that showed them the scar of the peat cuttings, superb views down the sound, and the ruined house. Their progress upset birds and panicked a ewe who took off at speed along a sheep track that spiralled around the hillside.

They talked about what they saw, not the question that was uppermost in Linda's mind: *'When can we leave?'* At the ruin Tom told tall tales of boyhood adventures, elaborate and implausible episodes she obligingly pretended to accept. Sometimes, she was sure, he was deliberately confabulating but she suspected he believed in the rest. Snippets of legend seemed caught up in these stories, like weed entangled in fishing nets.

Historical truths were hauled in too, such as the tale of the mariner marooned. A man had been sent ashore by his shipmates to beg provisions from some islanders. He found them all dead of the plague. When he shouted the news to his companions they recoiled, sailing away and abandoning him. In the fabled year and a day they returned and rescued him. Linda recognised the story because a Scottish writer had written a poem about the man's trials and solitude. The island was Mingulay, the southern tip of the archipelago. Tom shifted the action to his island.

It crossed her mind that he was testing her credulity, seeing how outlandish he might be before she challenged him. She was being treated like a fool but it was better not to offer critical comments on the stories. Stories were stories, that was the value of them. Their origins, and whether they contained facts, were immaterial. Just as poems meant one thing or several, so did stories.

Tom had been caustic about her taped poem, objecting to the tender blurring that developed a simple contention into a sophisticated piece of writing with several layers of meaning. He had not been comfortable with a poem that could mean one thing or another or preferably both. But here he was, performing the same trick himself. When he said such and such a thing had happened on the island, it meant only that it was imaginable and wouldn't it have been awful or wonderful? The nine-year-old Tom went fishing with a little rod, hoping for flounders, and caught a massive shark; and his mother fed them all on shark steaks for the rest of the holiday. Or someone had been marooned on an island of corpses, and lived to tell the tale. To do other things too, no doubt, but it was always telling the tale that was mentioned. Stories were important.

Tom touched her arm. 'Hey, wake up.'

She slipped her arm through his, managed to laugh at being caught in reverie while he was working to amuse her. 'Sorry, I was miles away.'

And oh how she wished she were, instead of simulating pleasure and going through the motions of companionship, and struggling with variable success to hide her true feelings. She drew him away from the ruin, thinking to lead them down to the boat. By completing the circuit of the island, they would come close to the jetty and the question of leaving would arise quite naturally. That way she would not seem to be pestering him to go and he would have no excuse for stubbornness.

Before they had gone very far he slowed, then came to a halt. There was a rock a few yards ahead of them, a steep slope on their right and then the sea and the inevitable scattering of islands. Apart from that there was nothing to look at. She wondered whether he had seen a bird or small creature, there seemed no other reason for choosing this spot to stop.

'What is it?' She kept her voice low, afraid of frightening away whatever it was.

'If you go up on that rock I'll show you.'

More whispering. 'No, come on, tell me.'

He refused to say.

To get it over with, Linda scrambled up to the rock. It was a modest affair jutting out of the hillside a few yards above the track and it was easy to get on to it. A brave plant had taken root on the exposed top and was forcing its roots down into a fissure, cracking the rock. On the other side of the rock the hill curved away as usual. There was nothing of special interest, not on the rock or to be seen from it. Puzzled she looked round for Tom. He was where she had left him, maybe a little closer. She waved.

'Aren't you coming up?'

He said something comical about being afraid of heights. While she was laughing, he pointed the camera at her.

'Number eight.' The words screamed in her brain. There was no one else in the frame, she was a laughing woman photographed alone against an empty sky. Possibly the shot included a strip of unidentifiable hillside, but that was all. *'Number eight.'*

Linda jumped off the rock and sped downhill, fast. She heard him thudding along behind her. She had no idea where she was going, where might be safe, or what she would say to him when he caught up with her as he was bound to do. His footing was more certain than hers and this was his island, he knew it and its peculiarities.

When she reached a fork she had to choose whether to dash on or to double back on a lower track and make for the beach. Which beach? An island is all beaches. She glimpsed the jetty and realised where she was. Turning sharp left, she plunged down the lower track.

He was waiting for her. He had anticipated her decision and slithered from the higher level to the lower, arriving in time to cut her off.

Tom flung out his arms to bar her way. He was fooling. 'Got you!'

And so was she, disguising horror and panic with playfulness. She tried to duck beneath his arm or to loop around out of his reach. He caught her easily.

'The boat's leaving,' she said, making a game of it. 'The tide's turning and the boat's leaving and we have to run. Race you to the boat.'

But he did not respond, except to clutch her arm tight and make running off impossible. Energy drained from her. She was defeated. Meeting his eyes, Linda feared he understood what had alarmed her. Without a word or an accusation, she had given away what was in her mind. A moment's panic and, for all her guile, she had ruined everything.

His next words proved it as he went straight to the point. 'You're not usually camera shy.'

'Let go.' She wrenched her arm free. But she did not flee, the energy had gone.

'That was a good shot.'

She swung away from him, refusing to listen.

He said: 'I got the essence of Linda, all that air and freedom and you looking happy to be alive.'

'Stop it, Tom.'

'It's true. I caught you exactly as you like to be. Space and freedom and happiness. Isn't that what you came for?'

But she pushed by and went down the hill, plodding, breathing hard, miserable and scared.

A flurry of gulls took to the air as she reached the jetty. They screamed like a warning, then buzzed about her head. She flapped her arms and bawled at them. 'I know, I *know.*' They did not go but became circling bodyguards travelling with her, protecting her with themselves.

She wished she could fly. Or that the revolutions of the birds could twirl her away over the water at the eye of a benign little whirlwind. Or that by clinging to a pair of scaly yellowy legs she could ride beneath umbrella wings.

Abruptly they deserted her. They floated down to the fishy feast she had gatecrashed, a mess of bones and flesh on grey stones.

Linda humped her bag into the boat and once more weighed her chances with the engine and the currents. The tide was higher now, the boat level with the stretch of the jetty where it was moored. Casting off had ceased to be a problem because she would be able to hold on to the rim of the boat while boarding instead of relying on the rope. At least, she thought so. She slackened the rope, slightly. One of the bigger waves crashed against the jetty, the boat bounded from her, and icy water penetrated her clothes.

Water sloshed in the bottom of the boat, it lapped around her bag. Tom's, on the jetty, was wet too. She carried his a foot or two from the water's reach. Handling it reminded her that she had not transferred the album. Wondering whether this was a good opportunity, Linda cast around for him.

At first she did not spot him but then discovered him on the rocks, the ones that featured in the made up story about the shark. From where he sat he had an excellent view of everything she did. Apparently, he was content to watch her escape although it meant she was marooning him.

'I'm going,' she yelled, not knowing or caring whether he heard the words.

He stayed there. She stepped into the boat, thinking: *'Well, that's the decision made. Now I'm committed. I've got to do it.'*

First though she needed to scoop out the water. She had earlier noticed an empty can in the boat and supposed it was kept for that purpose. Linda began to scoop. She was cold, damp and nervous but it felt good to be doing something positive instead of fretting about what Tom might have done in the past or what he might be scheming.

When she had been baling for several minutes the boat was as dry as she would be able to get it, but the next wave swamped it. Water slapped down on her back, rivulets ran over her bag, and the puddle was recreated. Smothering wails of frustration, she glanced over to the rocks to see how Tom was treating her setback. Tom had gone.

She heard his footsteps on the jetty. Forcing bravery, she grinned up at him and brandished the can. 'I'm baling out.'

'Not very successfully by the look of it.'

'There was another wave.'

'There always is.'

Rapidly, wildly, she began scooping again, racing against the inevitable rush of water that would wipe out her efforts. Behind her back she heard Tom say: 'It looked as though you were trying to go without me.'

Her face was flushed with exertion, a pinkness that could be mistaken for guilt. 'No, no of course not. I called to you. I asked you to come.'

'You were trying to go without me.'

Despite herself she had a rush of ill temper. 'I've been begging you to come for hours.'

'You were going without me. Look, you dumped my bag here. You didn't put it in the boat, did you?'

She was fast losing her battle to keep calm. The boat was juddering, and she detested the feeling of helplessness that motion caused her. Standing, she had one hand clenched on the can and the other useless because there was nothing to grab to keep her balance. Water washed around her shoes.

She snapped back at him. 'No, Tom, I didn't put yours in the boat. It was going to get wet, like mine, wasn't it? I wanted you to come and do it when we were ready to go. So come on, get in and let's be away.'

Without waiting for his answer she bent and scooped at the puddle, flinging water over the side, anyhow, not noticing whether the wind carried it away or threw it back at the boat. The faster she cleared it, the sooner it would be reasonable for Tom to get on board.

'You couldn't have gone,' he said.

'What?'

'I said you couldn't have gone without me.'

'I heard what you said. What does it mean?'

He dangled a key. 'You can't start the engine without this.'

Her eyes went from the key to the knob on the engine and back to the key. Now she understood his indifference as he had watched her antics from his perch on the rocks.

He said: 'I suppose you might know a way to do it. After all, you know how to cross the wires on a car engine, don't you?'

'Give it to me.' A chance, just a chance. She held out her open palm.

Tom ran a few steps backwards. Childishly taunting her, she thought, but then the next big wave arrived and foaming water was chasing him up the jetty. The puddle in the boat was twice as deep. Linda flung down the can and clambered ashore.

'This is hopeless.'

Tom pointed to the sky. 'Well, look at it. What do you expect?'

While she had been preoccupied the sky over the main island had changed. Gone were the wispy clouds feathering the crags. Mountains had vanished in a threatening confusion of rock and cloud. White galleon clouds were beating down the sound. One after another islands changed their hue, from gold to grey. Then it was the turn of Tom's island. The glorious day was to end in a storm.

11

She crouched by the window of her cell waiting for a second fishing boat to sail into view from the direction of the harbour but none came. She was there when a flurry of rain spattered down on the beach and when the wind dried the pebbles and when the first evening lights flared yellow on the distant shore. The air was dense and darkening, and when she eventually turned away she saw how shadows had gathered in the corners of the room and diminished the space around her. Stiffly she got to her feet, holding on to a wall to keep her balance.

To her amazement she saw the door gaping. Secretly, behind her back, some time in the heart-breaking hours since the fishing boat had sailed by, the door had been opened. She was afraid. The miraculous thing had happened but she was nervous about going out. Instead of flying to freedom she peered at the black space. Then she took a tentative step towards it, her feet dragging and clumsy because of the hours bent beneath her on the cold stone.

After two more steps she was less certain about the door and her doubt held her back. If it was another of her fantasies, then she wanted to savour it a little longer. There was another reason for caution too: the cellar door was not the only one separating her from the world. Beyond it lay a flight of steps up to the door into the lobby, and she did not know whether it was possible for that one to be locked against her. She took another step.

Shadows swirled around her. She felt herself falling and lunged forward, groping for a hand hold. Her outstretched hands touched wood where she had seen only a black void. For a few minutes she stood there, flattening her body against the door, her cheek resting on its smooth surface. Then she slid down and huddled on the floor in front of it. Her wariness had proved wise and she felt clever not to have trusted her eyes. Also there was a curious comfort in finding the door in its familiar position.

From beneath the door came a slight current of air that she did not remember. On her first day she had examined the door minutely and there had definitely been no draught. It might, she thought, be caused by a change of wind direction down the kitchen chimney, or else mean a window had blown open. She aimed to find out by regularly checking the air flow. It was important to her to do so because even the slightest changes assumed enormous significance in her shrunken world.

Some while later she decided to count the paces around the room again, preliminary to trying another sum. The total was higher than anything she had arrived at before. This discovery excited her as it suggested her prison was expanding. How interesting, she thought, that after their earlier effort to crowd in on her the walls were now moving back. To determine how much space she had gained, she began another circuit of the room. By now the shadows had thickened into a velvety blackness and so, to be sure that she counted correctly, she trailed her fingers along the walls.

Gritty stone skimmed beneath her fingertips, followed by a long section of rough plaster and then wood. She had no sense of her own movement but an impression of the room swivelling around her. When she registered stone for the second time she was mildly surprised but quickly realised that this was the trick: the room was duplicating its features rather than expanding each one. Duplicating? Ah no, she had come upon stone for the *third* time. Tripling, then. The room was already three times the size it used to be.

At this rate, she thought, it would soon swallow the beach and the waves would be lapping at it. What then? Must the sea curtail it or might it become a bridge carrying her across to the main island? Or, and this idea scared her, would it flood and sink and drown her?

Fingertips trailed over stone, plaster, a slab of wood, more stone. The fantastic room repeated itself. She could see nothing of its shape but her hands described it perfectly and she hurried after them, walking crabwise with both hands pawing the walls. And she was counting, losing count, consoling herself that slips were unimportant because it was no longer the number of paces that governed her but the number of repeats. Stone, plaster and wood.

Suddenly she burst into laughter, a terrible laughter that reverberated in the vast cavern the room had become. Her noise echoed in its high roof and rebounded from its walls of stone and plaster and wood. Before the cacophony had faded she repeated the laugh and then the room was repeating it too. Febrile and tiring, unable to complete the circuit, she stumbled on. What had been thrilling was turning sinister. She came to a full stop and listened for a silence that troubled her. There ought to be a creaking or a cranking, something to signal the slotting in of an extra wall of rock, of plaster or of wood. But no, the room was expanding without an audible clue to its methods. This bothered her very much. Even the most famous silent engines were no such thing and yet here she was in the midst of an activity that was being carried on in utter silence.

When the room had been contracting there was a definite squeezing noise. She remembered it distinctly. It was like . . . No, she did not have an apt simile this time. If pushed, she thought, she would have to explain it was like the sigh of a lemon being squeezed.

Now her ears were filled with the soft sounds of breathing, a regular pulsing breath. At once she was satisfied. This was precisely what she would have expected to hear from a room that was growing: a deep inhalation, a pause while expansion took place, and then a murmur of relaxation. The rhythm was comforting, soothing, reminiscent of something else although she could not imagine what, except of course for a person or an animal breathing.

Her counting had gone completely awry. She sat down right where she was, leaned her back against the wall and wondered what to do. There were two obvious options. Either she could start counting from where she was, although if she did that her total would be wildly inaccurate, or she could turn around and go back to the beginning and start again. It was a difficult choice and she spent a long time over it. There was also another possibility to consider: she could abandon her attempt to count. This was the most attractive course because it excused her from fighting on against increasingly unfavourable odds. On the other hand, it meant trudging back to her starting point and that was a long way back.

She sighed and the sigh echoed around the great hall of a room. Next she became aware again of the room's own breathing, only this time it was less like gasps and exhalations and more like the shushing sound of heavy curtains swishing across a window. But no, not curtains, it was less a clothy sound than the woosh of a besom over dusty stone. For an instant she relived the morning she leaned from a Mediterranean balcony to watch a headscarved woman sweeping night from a sunlit square.

146

Perturbed, she strained to hear which part of the cellar the sweeper was sweeping. The floor was dusty, therefore it was logical that someone should sweep it, but she wished she had understood earlier that she had company. She cocked her head and listened. Over there, she decided, that was where it was coming from. Well, now that she knew, she would go over and ask the sweeper the dimensions of the room and by what mysterious device it was enlarging itself and whether the process was finite.

Her face puckered in a frown because she suspected there were other questions she ought to put but they were escaping her. Never mind, these were the crucial ones. How big is the room? How big will it get? How does it grow?

Her legs were too feeble to get her upright so she wriggled from sitting to crouching and then settled for a crawl. With utmost concentration she slid towards the sound of the broom. Once she was away from the wall, orientation became hopelessly difficult. She could not pinpoint the sweeper's position. She called but the sweeper was apparently unable to hear and the brushstrokes carried on without a break in their rhythm. Frustration brought her to the verge of tears.

She worked it out: as the sweeping was getting no closer, and as she had not encountered anyone while she was edging along the walls, the sensible thing to do was to return to the place where she had been sitting. If she continued along the walls from that point, sooner or later she was bound to meet the sweeper.

With supreme care she revolved until she was confident she was facing back the way she had come. Then she crawled to a wall. She lined up parallel with it, her right shoulder next to the wall just as it had been when she was walking. She moved off.

Progress was slower because now that she was crawling she needed to keep reaffirming her position by pausing and stroking a hand on the wall. In this way she passed along one plaster wall and then a second. On the next run of wall she noticed a draught and her right hand found a gap beneath a slab of wood. Scuttling on she came to the wall of rock. This was inconvenient since it was not straight and smooth like the other walls and she bumped her head where it jutted into the cellar. Beyond it she made an intriguing discovery. Immediately the rock finished there was a change of surface and, running her hand up it to investigate, her arm shot away into a cavity. Bringing her palm down slowly she rested it on a high step.

A flight of steps, she supposed, and she enjoyed the way a flight suggested a break for freedom. Her other bright thought was that this solved the puzzle of the sweeper who had been hard to locate because she was not actually in the room but sweeping the steps or perhaps a room above. Then the flight and the broomstick and the sweeper from the sunlit morning square became snarled up together in a delightful dream of sailing through the air to the main island.

Hoisting herself on to the step she groped for a second one but lost her balance and tumbled down and had to mount again. The sequence repeated itself and she rapidly became confused about the number of steps she had climbed.

While she was on the step which she took to be the third or possibly the fourth, something alarming happened. A ghostly whiteness transformed the room and there, lying across the floor, was the sweeper's broomstick. She hurled herself down the steps and scrabbled for the stick. As she got to it, it vanished. The room was blacker than ever.

She howled, alone and terrified and tormented. And when she broke off raging and stared into the unyielding darkness of her prison, she noticed that the sweeper had gone away. The sound of bristles on stone had stopped. All she could hear was the wind whispering to the sea and telling tales among the rocks.

12

While the storm was blowing around the island, Tom and Linda took refuge in the house. It was cold, unpleasant and filled with the noise of the sea battering the shore and the rain pelting the windows.

'I do wish we could light the fire,' she said, just as she had said it the previous evening.

'In this wind? We'd be smoked out.'

'Oh, I hadn't thought of that.'

'We'd never get the chimney warm enough for it to draw. Besides, it wouldn't do us any good. A peat fire keeps you waiting before it's prepared to push out much heat.'

In a way it was a comforting remark, underlining that they would be off the island at the first chance. Linda avoided mentioning that they would not be enduring all this if he had not fiddled around and delayed them. She wondered exactly when he had noticed the distant sky changing and sending bad weather their way.

She got him to light the heater. He did it with a show of reluctance, telling her: 'There isn't a lot of fuel for it, you know. And we're low on matches.'

'I was hoping not to be here much longer.' She followed up with a wry smile.

He took another sweater from his bag, saying she ought to put on extra layers if the cold was getting to her.

'I can't,' she said. 'I've already changed out of the things that got wet when I was hit by the waves. I didn't bring many clothes, remember.'

'Have this then. I've got my grey one in here somewhere.' He gave her the sweater and routed around for the grey.

Linda pulled the sweater over her head. It smelled of him, of sweat and smoke, whisky, the sea and the island. *'This is what it's like when people die,'* she thought. *'They linger in the smells of their*

149

clothes, each unwashed garment a catalogue of "last times". The last time they cooked food or mowed grass or opened a fizzing can of beer. The last time they rode an open boat through sea spray, or stood in diesel fumes, or were too hot and wiped the sweat from their faces with a sleeve.'

Tom had become very still. She stopped exploring the idea and concentrated on him, guessing how he was going to tell her the album had disappeared and choosing what she ought to say in reply.

'Something's missing,' he said.

'Can't you find the grey sweater?'

He raised the sweater to show it was not that.

Linda asked: 'What then?'

'The photograph album.'

So there was to be no pretence after all, no ambiguity or obliqueness. The album, that's what he said. He had never referred to it until this moment, and she had been pretending not to know of its existence.

She made her choice, asked a practical, skirting around the issue question. 'When did you last have it?'

He shrugged. 'Have you seen it?'

The lie. 'No.'

'A green album, are you sure you haven't seen it?'

'Perhaps you left it in the hire car.'

He tapped his bag with a toe. 'No, it was in here.'

'Well, try the bedroom. Perhaps it fell out and you left it behind.'

Looking doubtful, he went into the bedroom.

Linda did not look in that direction. She could not bear to know whether he was searching or squinting at her through the crack in the door jamb to see what she was up to. By now the unlikelihood of the album having been beneath her bag by mischance that morning was glaring. *'He planted it there,'* she thought, *'to make sure I saw it. Ever since we came here he's been taunting me.'*

Tom returned to the kitchen, saying he had not found it. Then: 'You're sure you didn't gather it up with your stuff?'

Too quickly she said not. 'I'd have noticed.'

It was far too late to hand it over, it had to stay where it was until she could get rid of it. Her eyes scoured the room for hiding places. At the end of the room was the cooker, an old-fashioned thing on a shelf near the sink. Linda regarded it as a hiding place. Failing that there was the curtained shelf beneath the sink, or else the food cupboard. A slim folder slipped behind a row of tins would be perfectly hidden. Unless, she corrected herself, they decided to eat anything. In that event it would be swiftly discovered. She continued scouring the room for hiding places.

Tom, who was peering out of the window, said: 'It's clearing.'

'Enough?'

'Not yet but I'll keep an eye on it.' Then: 'It's very odd where it's got to. Are you absolutely sure . . .'

'Yes.'

Linda joined him at the window. The view was less encouraging than she expected, dark and rainy. 'Oh, I thought you meant it was better than this.'

'Look to the west, that's the way the weather comes. It's definitely growing lighter.'

'Hmm.' Unconvinced, she let another sigh escape. Her breath misted the pane.

Tom nosed around the house, muttering about the missing album. He even checked the cellar. Hearing him on his way down the steps to it, she held her breath. Was this her opportunity? Her bag was on the other side of the room from where she sat. With three stealthy strides she reached it. Then the zip was skimming back and her hand was slipping inside.

Oven or sink shelf? The distances were equal and he had not bothered to open the oven door or whisk aside the curtain. But her next thought was that they were silly places. If the album turned up in one of those, it would prove it had been deliberately tucked out of sight. One did not accidentally toss a folder into an oven and shut the door on it. As for the sink shelf, was he supposed to think she had caught the album up with the bottle of washing up liquid and plonked them side by side? No, they were ridiculous places.

Tom's bag then, back to her first plan. This stood open a couple of yards from her own so it was feasible to make the switch. Later, when he found it, it would appear a case of having missed the very thing he was hunting, which was what people did all the time.

Tom's feet scraped on the stones of the cellar. There was grit and sand down there, one could not move without making noise. She had time, then, to make the switch.

But she could not put her hand on the album. Her notebook with the new poem was on top of her clothes, but her sponge bag had set off on its travels and the album too had worked its way down.

Linda plundered the bag, broke off and listened again. Footsteps on stone steps. In two strides she was at the window, pleading with the sky to clear and the sea to calm. As he came into the room she made a weak joke about her supplications.

She began to feel hysterical, seeing herself as one of the heroines of melodrama who fly about the stage in badly concealed panic, with an incriminating letter to hide or to search for. Doubly incompetent, she had not only failed to pick a good hiding place for her version of the letter, she had mislaid it too.

Or had she? Tom had been alone with the two bags at various times since they had sheltered from the storm. He could easily have dipped into her bag and . . .

Tom came into the kitchen. He went straight to the outside door, opened it and walked a little way until he had a view of the jetty. Rain had petered out and the air that blew through the house was sweet and filled with hope.

'Maggie?'

She went to the door. Light was breaking through cloud here and there, daubing the sea and mountains with warm colours. Waves dashed against rocks and spray arced high over them. The birds had gone and the boat was tearing at the rope, straining to go too.

Tom said: 'There's quite a swell. Do you think you can face that?'

Of course she said yes.

In about fifteen minutes he had baled out the boat and came up to the house to tell her it was time to go. She was ready, with her jacket on over the layers of sweaters. Her pocket was flat, the sheet of newspaper in her bag. The baling had also allowed her time to retrieve the album. With Tom out of the way she could have put it in his bag or hidden it in the house but she chose to keep it, thinking of it as evidence she ought to safeguard. Also, she wanted to study those faces again and see whether she could learn anything from them.

Tom got the engine going and they cast off. The sea seemed alarmingly rough before they were clear of the jetty, and Linda dreaded to think what she must endure before they arrived on the other side. But she was silent about her fears because it was right to leave the island. Although the weather might become calmer yet, it could worsen. Whichever it did, Tom would not cross in the dark. He did not know the skerries or the currents well enough to attempt that, he had said so.

They passed the end of the jetty. The house lolled against the hill and then it was out of sight as they swung in the direction of the distant harbour. Drawing away from the island they saw its shape, the scar on its hill and a couple of sheep wandering across the spoiled patch.

The boat lurched. Water slapped over the side. Linda's grip tightened on the wooden slat where she sat. She grimaced at the water swishing up and down in the bottom of the boat. *'How many of those make the difference between floating and sinking? Shut up. Oh, shut up. You mustn't think like that . . .'*

Another wave splashed aboard. The sky was getting brighter but the sea was seething. She gazed at Tom's island but it was not decreasing in size, merely changing shape. The pale rectangular buildings on the main island remained as diminutive as ever.

When another wave swamped them, Tom shouted across demanding that she bale. She had been putting it off, praying she need not loosen her hold on the seat. Disguising her dislike and her queasiness, Linda picked up the tin and scooped.

She was crouching doing this when the boat was buffeted so fiercely that she automatically let the tin fall and grabbed the side of the boat. Tom was struggling to keep his balance. She backed on to her seat, where she could keep her weight steady and not add to their problems by tilting the craft.

Tom, she realised, was not much good with boats. It came as a surprise and ought not to have done. Yes, he had talked about them because his island holidays had involved boat journeys and at home in the southern seaside town he had played around boats. But he would not have been in charge in those days and, anyway, she distrusted many of his claims. Despite all that, she had never doubted his ability to get them across the sound to safety.

The boat rocked, threatening to fling them out. It was behaving like a creature out of control. The puddle of water around their feet was deepening. Tom shouted again that she must bale.

While she was doing it there was a choking noise and the engine cut out. She saw her look of horror reflected on Tom's face. Neither of them spoke. There was the sound of the sea whipped by the wind, of waves bashing against the boat, and of nothing else.

Linda scooped frantically. When she looked up again, Tom was whitefaced, bent over the engine. She remembered the mower and tried to think what the instructions were for using that, and then dismissed the whole thing as a digression. She looked beyond Tom to the main island. Buildings that dotted its shore were no bigger, no nearer. She glanced over her shoulder and saw Tom's island and its sentinel rocks. The boat had travelled a negligible distance in all the dreadful time they had been afloat.

A wave caught them and pushed them away. They were going where they were pushed. They were drifting. Her eyes went again to the rocks. She began measuring the distance.

'Tom . . .'

He grunted but did not raise his head from the engine.

She said: 'We're drifting towards those rocks.'

'All part of the package tour. Didn't you know?'

'There's no need to be sarcastic.'

At that moment he got a squeak out of the engine. Half a minute later, it happened again.

Linda was contemplating bladderwrack, thick fleshy tendrils groping up at them through the water. The waves were pushing them on, and the weed was reaching out knobby fingers to draw them in. Ahead floated a mat of the stuff, jostled by the waves. She knew very little about sea weeds but she knew they grew on rocks. Beyond the mat lay gleaming stone in a haze of spume.

She wondered how it would be. Would the boat become snagged on the mat of weed and held fast until the tide rose and it floated free? Or would the rocks beneath the weed rip the keel out of the boat before then? Or would one of the more energetic waves hurl the boat to splinter on the bare rocks?

The engine revived again, coughed, struggled gamely to keep going. Tom shouted to Linda to hold tight and then he jerked the boat away from danger. He shouted something else but she did not hear what. The engine was making a ragged, unreliable noise. There was more weed, then she looked down on rock, and then there was white water signalling other hazards.

He did not head out into the sound again, he took the boat back to the jetty. He had to.

'I despise people who are violent,' he said. 'Have you ever known me to be violent?'

He was scathing and his words caught her by surprise. It was another of his conversational hops. She did not understand what she had said to get him on to this tack.

In her head she argued back: *I don't know you. You're too many people, I don't know which is the real Tom.*

But she was silent, busying herself at the stove, stirring the contents of a can of soup. She was too hungry and weary for confrontation. It made her nervous that he sounded serious but she lacked the energy to twist him round to playful.

As soon as the boat had limped alongside the jetty, she had raided the stock of tins in the food cupboard. Soon, she supposed, once she was fed and more comfortable, she would agonise about being stuck on the island for a second night. So far she felt only relief at being on dry land after having come close to shipwreck and probably drowning.

While she was cooking, Tom lit the heater and poured whisky, saying her drink was waiting on the table for her. But she was more concerned about eating and continued stirring. It was then that he made those remarks about violence.

Eventually, satisfied the soup was smooth and heating gently, she turned away from the stove. What she saw shocked her rigid. He was seated at the table turning the pages of the photograph album. The tension in her body became an ache and she had to force herself to go near him, sit at the table and carry on normally.

Her hand wavered as she lifted her glass. Whisky scorched her throat and glowed inside her. She relished the sensation for a second or two before asking the question it would be absurd not to ask.

'Who are they, Tom?'

'Women I knew.' He flicked back to the beginning and went through them again.

From Linda's perspective they were on their heads. One, the fair perm. Two, the big shoulder pads and puffed up hair. Three, the youngster in cardigan and leggings. Four, the elfin blonde. Five, the bobbed hair and T shirt. Six, the one she believed was Anita Gayner. Seven, the long-haired brunette in the green shirt.

She heard herself say: 'Tell me their names.'

Her temerity startled her and she wished she had put a less specific question. If only she had made a light-hearted sally about them being ex-lovers, then she would have offered a loophole for the truth to slip through. But she had begged names.

'*He'll make them up,*' she thought. '*Of course he will, he's always toying with people's names. It'll be all right because Tom will lie.*'

She took another searing mouthful of whisky and depended on the lie.

Tom pointed to number one, the woman with the fair curls that looked like a perm. 'Ellen,' he said. The pages turned, the names were chanted. 'Carol. Jenny. Louise. Patsy. Anita. Pauline.'

The room shimmered. Linda was trembling. He had not done it,

155

he had not lied. He had said Anita, and if Anita was correct, then so were the others. If . . .

Tom leaned towards her. She pressed back against her chair, her breath uneven and too loud. Gently he took her glass from her and refilled it.

She struggled to say something noncommittal, unchallenging, something that would not lead to revelations. Knowledge was danger. If he had decided to taunt her with the details, she had to prevent him doing so.

He said: 'The soup.'

She stared, mystified.

He got up and turned off the heat beneath the pan. She noticed the room had filled with a steamy oxtail warmth. He was behind her. She was frightened of that and, swivelling in her chair, she kept guard. He was pouring soup into bowls. The very thought of food choked her. Her tumbler chinked against her teeth as she swallowed another sip of whisky.

'Anita. He didn't lie, he said Anita.'

It became a refrain in her mind, until it gave way to that earlier one: *'Number eight. Number eight.'*

At last she managed, in a reasonably casual way: 'Family, friends or lovers?'

A bowl of soup was placed in front of her. Hunger reasserted itself. She raised a spoonful to her lips while awaiting his answer.

She got his wicked look. 'I collect people.'

He ate quickly and then said he was going to examine the engine before darkness fell. Linda finished her soup alone.

The photograph album lay beside his empty bowl. She could not take her eyes away from it. When she had finished eating she opened it, going straight to the woman he had called Anita. Her hand hesitated for a second and then she drew the photograph from its plastic envelope. On the back was written: Anita Gayner, Dorris Castle, and a date two years ago.

Linda looked at the woman's laughing face, at the shape of an island in the background, at the expanse of sky, and the tops of pine trees.

'The tower,' she thought. *'He photographed her on one of the towers.'*

'Come on up,' he had called down to Linda when they were at the castle together, but she had refused.

Again she thrust away the temptation to run over it all in her head. It seemed more important to skirt fresh dangers and to keep a companionable relationship going until morning when they could have another shot at leaving. If the boat engine was not to be trusted, they would have to attract attention and be fetched.

She slotted the photograph into the album, then she drew out number one. On the reverse was written Ellen Day, Northumberland, and a date ten years ago. Number two was Carol Spencer, dated eight years back. Then Jenny Woodville, six years. Louise Denner, four. Patsy Brett, three. Pauline Morris was almost a year ago.

The only one she recognised was Jenny Woodville, not the woman's appearance but her name. When Jenny Woodville had gone missing, it had struck a chord with Linda because she had been at school with a Penelope Woodville. Penny and Jenny were close enough for her to register the name.

She remembered lots of things about Penny, such as that she was a snob who trawled for family connections with Elizabeth Woodville, one of the queens of England. On a bus once, Penny had confided her young brother's intention to christen his first daughter Elizabeth and thus continue family tradition. The brother was about twelve at the time, not an age to be troubling about past or future, and Linda had not believed a word of it.

As for Jenny Woodville, Linda knew nothing but her name. She was the youngest in the album, the one with her hair looped up in an untidy knot, the one wearing leggings and a long knitted cardigan. Slightly gap-toothed, she had a cheeky smile and appeared a lively sort of character.

Linda slipped the faces back into their plastic envelopes, thinking that Tom had consigned them to the past when he named them. 'Women I knew,' he had said, not 'Women I know.'

Then she washed up and just as she finished, he came, saying: 'It's working all right now.'

'Did the water affect it?'

'Probably muck in the fuel. I don't really know, they can be temperamental.'

'Well, let's hope it's in a good mood in the morning.'

'Pray for fine weather,' he said.

For some reason her memory chose that moment to flash her images of them standing in a steep valley hemmed in by rock.

'Listen,' he had said, and he had roared 'Maggie'. An echo came pinging back to them.

Laughing, she had corrected him by shouting 'Linda'.
But there was no echo.
'You've disappeared,' he had said.

13

Dawn dappled the sea with pink. From the window of her cell it looked as though drifts of rose petals were floating by. She smiled a lazy smile at the image of herself escaping on a gigantic rose petal, a latterday Celtic heroine whose fate was entwined with the sea and flowers.

Yawning she leaned against the wall beside the window and looked obliquely out at the new day. In the dusky corners of the room faces clamoured but she was too weary to acknowledge them. She decided to pretend she did not know they were there. Without looking she could name them: Rusty, the witchy colleague from the bookshop, who had not been duped by her ruse about an Italian holiday; Jerome, who had been fooled and made her presents of Italian travel books; Helen, who could have been in Turkey but had not gone because she dreaded solo holidays; Janet, who sent brief, adaptable postcards; Kathy, who had organised one glorious Tuscan holiday and then ruled out repetition by falling in love; Anita Gayner, who had been at the castle but not left it alive.

She wriggled, to rub her itching back against the wall. Outside the rose petals were being gilded. On the beach was a flattish smudge that used to be a mound of wool and before that a sheep. A row of gulls lined up like targets on the rocks.

Rusty was the one who had been sweeping with a broom during the night, she thought. It was typical of her to be a quiet knowing presence, perpetually busy and efficient. Helen would not have done it, she would have been fussing about her clothes: country or town for a visit to an island cell?

She sneaked a glance across the room. Her mother was lining teapots along a shelf and Jerome was removing them and putting up books, and her mother was removing the books and putting back the teapots. She saw it all in the split second before she turned away

159

again. Let them do it, let them get on with it, what did it matter? The tide would come and the tide would go and the teapots would come and the teapots would go. And what did any of it matter?

She felt she ought to say as much to Jerome because he was warm and uncomplicated and would not know how tough and intransigent and relentlessly kind her mother could be. But no, she would let him find out for himself, it was not fair to interfere.

Out on the water the rose petals were being submerged in gold, sinking and drowning until the sea was the sea again and not a flowing garden after all. She was not entirely happy about the lapse into reality, she preferred the beauty and the conceit of the roses. Besides, how could she look forward to sailing away on a gigantic rose petal if all the rose petals had been drowned in gold? Gold did not float, everyone knew that.

When she next looked across the room its shadiness was spangled with gold like brilliant autumn leaves falling, falling, falling. The sight made her catch her breath and think *'Could I have been here as long as that?'* But she did not know as long as what exactly because she had lost count of days and time and all she had left to measure with was the creeping of the water and the coursing of the sun. What of the moon? she wondered. Nights had been cloudy and the moon a mere curl of citrus peel. She had not been enchanted by moonlight.

She looked at the enchantresses. Rusty and her mother were in cahoots over the teapots, and there too was Helen, dressed for one of her charity committee meetings and speaking in that fluting manner of hers, begging a cup of tea, as it happened.

Swinging her head away before they noticed her, she kept out of it. It rankled, though, that they were so unconcerned about her. Ought they not to be comparing notes, something along the lines of: 'Where did Linda say she was going? Italy? Oh, I see, she sent you a postcard. Well, that was nice of her. What did she write? Was that all? No, I'm not criticising, it's just that "Wish you were here" is rather hackneyed for someone who thinks of herself as a poet. Used to, anyway. Ah yes, a joke, of course, being ironical.'

The voice was insistent and she shook her head to clear her mind. Through the bars the gulls were making their first inspection of the beach for that day. A big wave stirred them into agitated loops. She laughed at their indignity.

If one came near enough, she thought, she could snatch it through the bars, teach it to talk and send it to fetch help. She frowned, knowing she had that wrong, but in seconds the puzzle unravelled. It was Bran who taught a bird to talk. Her own scheme was a note lashed to a bird's leg with strands of her hair. Loose strands or plaited? She could not recall which she had settled on but she was convinced the distinction was crucial.

Thinking it over, she began to pull out her hair, selecting long strands from her scalp and laying them side by side on the right leg of her trousers. By shifting her leg slightly she could make them shiver with colour. When she had married Richard she used to dye her hair but he said it looked wrong and it was stupid to waste money on it when your own hair was all right anyway. So she had given up, which was less bother than trying to commandeer the bathroom for the amount of time the shampooing in, the setting and the rinsing demanded. A pity, she thought, that she had not taken it up again once she had her own flat because she had enjoyed playing with the colour. Today she was glad she had not succumbed to Tom's pressure to have it cropped.

She tweaked another hair. It was coarser than the others, coarse and white. She wondered how much of her hair had turned grey, and dragged a fistful round to look at it but the hair was dirty and the ends were dry and splitting and she thrust it back out of sight. One evening, when she was at college, she had trapped a leggy spider beneath a glass on the study floor and left it for Kathy, who was spider-brave, to deal with it. Kathy's way was to slip a sheet of paper beneath the glass and teeter out of doors with the terrible cargo. But this time when Kathy came the spider had turned white all over, and all the girls in the house had shrieked to see it fleeing down the garden into the night like its own ghost.

Did Anita Gayner's mousey hair turn white while she was incarcerated in the castle? Linda began to plait the hairs she had tugged from her scalp, holding them firmly between her lips. Her fingers fumbled and she had to stop and start over again. She was quite sure now that plaiting was necessary. When she had made the skinny plait she took the free end from her mouth and was disappointed to see the plait flopping apart. For a few minutes she considered how to prevent this happening and eventually drew another hair from her head and wrapped the end tightly and made a double knot in it. Then she anchored the other end in the same way. The result was less neat than she had envisaged: the plait was curved and uneven. But it would serve its purpose, she thought, and she coiled it in her pocket for safekeeping until she was ready to use it.

In the other pocket she found the wrapper from the peppermints. It surprised her that the peppermints were not there too. After she had hunted around she concluded she had eaten them. In halves and quarters, in crumbs and licks, they had all gone. The hunger too had gone. She suffered neither the pain of it nor the emptiness.

Perhaps, she thought, she had binged on the peppermints. It was hard to tell because her dreams were vivid and her waking thoughts vague and meandering. There were times when she could not sort out which was which. She scowled at the piece of paper in her hand and chased after a memory.

It came to her: she had been about to write a note, attach it to a bird and send the bird for help. Outside the birds were playing games with the creaming surf, leaping out of its way as it snatched at them, dropping down as it fell back and drew breath for another attack. Flirting with danger, they were as foolhardy as youths who ran with the bulls or rattled the cages of lions, or like herself being attracted to a man who collected victims.

A bird dived by the window and its wings dragged dark shapes across her floor. Ignoring the bird she watched the shadow wings, grabbing for them but missing. She was not the only one, in the corner of the room there was a flurry of arms. Anita Gayner was wearing her evening dress but the others were more casual. She knew them from their photographs. They began to murmur that he had taken their photographs.

'As a memento mori,' said a voice in her skull or perhaps in the room. She gave the women in the corner a caustic look but they smiled back with the faces from the album, all except for Anita who appeared wary. One of them, precarious on the rock wall, looked very like herself.

'How soon did you realise he had trapped you and left you to die?' asked the voice, and it might have been a question for Anita or for the others or for herself.

'The three birds of Rhiannon gave sleep to the living and could awaken the dead,' Anita said.

Jerome pushed a teapot aside and lifted a book down from a shelf. He was thumbing it, looking up a reference. 'Immuration,' he murmured, 'it was one of the ways they killed women. No blood, you see. No violence or mess.'

'Dust,' snapped Helen, brushing it from her fingers. 'Always dust.'

162

'He hated blood,' Linda said. 'When we hit the sheep, he refused to kill it.'

Jerome continued to read the book and seemed not to have heard her. He read out: 'The Victorians were fond of keeping locks of the hair of their dead. Often they plaited it and wore it as jewellery.'

Rusty said: 'All witches are black cats in disguise.' She took a crunching bite out of the digestive biscuit in her left hand.

Linda turned to her window. A figure eight was written in sheen on the water. It elongated until one looping end was near the rocks and the other was almost in touch with the far shore. A shining track, her eyes followed it to safety.

Then she closed her eyes and sat a while feeling the salt air blowing over her skin and the grittiness of sand on the floor of the cellar. Dust and silence. She wanted to ask the other women what they had done to survive and how long they had succeeded, but she was too tired to put questions or absorb answers. When a voice suggested that it was awful too for the people who were waiting for the missing ones, she did not trouble to reply. Rusty did though, saying: 'What interests me is all those people who deliberately go missing. A false destination, a false name and they're away.'

Linda lifted her hair from her shoulders and twisted it into a plait, wondering why it made her feel good to wear it that way. Then she clamped her hands over her ears and wriggled closer to the window. The brightness of early morning was fading. A cloud that had been hooked on a mountain peak had broken loose and was rolling down. A funereal cormorant posed on the rocks where the dog whelks were sucking life from anything that took their fancy. Birds were stalking about on the rocks. Amphibolite. Pegamatite. The gulls brought to mind the plait in her pocket and the note she ought to have ready. She smoothed out the sweet wrapper, snapped the emery board to make a point, scratched it down her arm to draw blood, and wrote her message. Although she planned to put her address and the date clearly at the top, she had no idea of the date and the only address she could muster was MacTwaddle's Island.

Stuck, she lay the note aside while she worked out what else to say. Help seemed a useful word. She wrote that in capitals and underlined it. Then she added three exclamation marks because they were also a sort of underlining and she needed to be certain the message was taken seriously. After that there was not too much space left and so she just wrote 'trapped in cellar', in very small letters, and signed it. She licked at the blood on her arm.

Setting the note down by the window, she waited for it to dry. The blood dried brown, it was blobbed where the paper had absorbed it, and the letters were as badly formed as a young child's. Dissatisfied, she argued whether to send it, afraid it would not be read as a cry for help but as the fakery of a child's game. But it was all she had, there was no more paper to make a second attempt and so it must be sent. Over on the rocks the gulls lined up, beaks to the wind, and let her choose which one to use as her emissary.

She selected the one who reminded her of the jeweller, her Gloucester neighbour. They shared a way of dipping their heads, the bird stabbing at air and the man bowing his prominent nose towards his teacup. Picturing his willow pattern china, she saw too the gold charms in the glass case he used as a tea table in the shop. Finally, she remembered the distressing story of robbery and death. Another image intervened, an image of Tom taking from her the postcard she had written to the jeweller and then walking towards a postbox on the other side of the street. With sudden insight she realised that Tom had not posted it. Naturally enough, he had taken charge of it to destroy it because it gave away her whereabouts.

This ought to have dawned on her sooner, she thought, but she had been sluggish and ready to be fooled about his intentions. Too lazy, too amenable, too preoccupied with her new resolutions about writing more, doing more and trusting more, she had been easy prey. All along she had been gulled by him. Well, that was long past. She had ceased to believe in accidents and blunders. Everything seemed contrivance. The delay about catching the tide, and the near calamity when the boat ran near the rocks. Each incremental closing of the trap, she blamed him for them all. She was outraged and she hankered for revenge. The figures in the shadows encouraged her.

'Faith, hope and clarity,' they insisted.

With the note and the plait ready, she spent the afternoon cooing to entice a gull. It soon stopped mattering whether or not the one that responded was the chosen one, the one with the jeweller's dipping head. She was prepared to adapt to any bird that ventured within an arm's length of her prison. The gulls did not come, they found more fascinating diversions on the beach. Shellfish needed to be dropped on rocks, stranded weed had to be picked over, there were fishy drifts of sand to patrol, and there was the hissing surf to challenge and cheat. They ignored her or perhaps they could not hear her. To her own ears her cries were weak and wavering.

Breaking off, she rested and watched the colours change on the mountains and shore line of the main island. Waves created shadows and shapes like a flotilla but she was used to their duplicity and refused to be roused. All the same, she decided to tie the note to one of her bars so that the flapping might catch an eye if anyone were looking. She could not guarantee staying on guard.

Using the emery board she poked a hole in the paper and threaded the plait through it. When it was tied, she secured the other end to the bar. The paper hung down like a flag on a breathless day. She jiggled it about but it was no good, the breeze was blowing in the wrong direction. The sun, however, was marching up the beach and before very much longer she could signal again.

Holding the tin, buffing it, she waited for the sun to come and the breeze to blow the right way. Waiting, always waiting. She tried to think about the different kinds of waiting but there was something nagging at her mind and although she was reluctant to give it her attention, in the end she had to. The women in the corner of the room were egging her on.

First she buckled the tin and wrenched it about and forced a damaged corner into a point. Then she scraped the point against the rock wall, this way and that, rhythmically like the sweeping of a besom on stone. She kept feeling the point to test whether her whetstone was effective and eventually she decided it was. Just then bars of sunlight fell across the floor and she had to go to the window and wave the tin about for a while. Once the bars had gone she returned to sharpening the corner of her tin.

She used the weapon to slash her arm. She deepened the skinny cut the emery board had made earlier and the blood oozed darkly along her forearm. For a second she studied the way it rolled and ran over her grubby skin. Then she felt the soreness and that made her give up staring and do what she had determined to do.

Going to the plain wall, the one where the plaster surface was broken only by the row of nails, she dipped a forefinger into the blood and began to write. The smell of blood and the shock of the injury made her feel faint. She wished she could kneel but she had to keep standing because she intended to write large clear letters that would survive and one day would be understood.

There was much to say but she was concise, partly because she feared collapsing before getting to the end. So she began with his name, Tom Hoby, in plain capital letters, her hand working with the sweep of a schoolteacher at a blackboard. Then she thought she

165

must get her own name, Linda Conway, down quickly because that was equally important. She left a deep gap below his and dipped her finger in the blood and smeared her name across the wall. Then she thought how to fill the gap. Words such as 'left me here to die', or 'abandoned me' or 'has killed eight women' sounded appropriate but were long. Her legs gave way.

Huddled at the foot of the wall she grappled with words, trying to compose a pithy accusation that was easy to write and unambiguous. Her fears were coming true: she was weak and she was not clear headed. On the other side of the room a woman in an evening dress was appealing to her with sad eyes. Linda dragged herself up, knelt, took a gout of blood on her fingertip and reached up to fill the gap between the two names. She wrote one word: 'Killed.'

Then she fell back and lay there, clutching her bleeding arm against her chest. The murmuring of birds became the murmuring of women's voices and she understood they approved. Their approval gave her strength and she crawled to the window and waved the tin, not caring that it was not very shiny because it was all scratched and it was splodged with blood. Her other arm hurt. Looking down she was alarmed to see the front of her jacket soaked red.

The blood confused her. She did not require it any more and yet there it was, a slight but persistent ooze. Pressing her arm against her chest again, hoping to stop the flow, she waved the tin a couple of times. It flew from her grasp and clattered down on some stones on the beach. For a minute she looked at it, dumbfounded, thinking that as it had escaped it was crazy for it to be lying there and not already on its way to the other island. Then she shrugged and turned into the room.

Blood trickled down her arm and dripped from her fingertips. It was a pity to waste it and so she wrote on the wall again. Below her name she put Anita Gayner, and beneath that she crammed Jenny Woodville. She squeezed in the others as best she could alongside these three. It concerned her that the names were out of order. She knew the order by heart: Ellen Day, Carol Spencer, Jenny Woodville, Louise Denner, Patsy Brett, Anita Gayner and Pauline Morris. To rectify the mistake, she wrote numbers beside the names.

After that there was nothing to do. She took up her usual place by the window and stared out, her mind far away and her eyes unseeing. From time to time she licked at the blood on her arm and once she decided she ought to bandage it to help it heal. But she could not see what to use as a bandage and by the time she thought a sock would probably do she realised that the flow had more or less dried up anyway.

He had hooked her, he had played her like a fish from the moment he saw her, and he would get away with it because he had got away with it seven times before. The black thought went round and round: she was dying, he had killed her and he would get away with it.

One day, when the echo of her heartbeat had long died away, the MacTwaddle family would come for their summer holiday and read the bloody script on the wall of their cellar. She drew scant comfort from the hope that he would be traced and punished. Thinking of the people he had called the MacTwaddles, she looked round to see what would meet their eyes as they pulled open the long locked door. Stepping inside, the first thing they would see was the wall with the row of nails and the bloody writing.

When she read her message, she plunged into utter despondency. Like the words on the scrap of paper, the ones on the wall had lost the ferocity of redness. They were dingy brown streaks, fading unevenly as the plaster sucked them dry. The word linking his name and hers was particularly misshapen and she had misspelled it. The message seemed to be 'Tom loves Linda'.

This travesty set her moaning, a song of wretchedness and woe. He hated blood and she had resorted to blood for her revenge, but she had managed only a mangled lovers' scrawl. Those other names, and those numbers, they conveyed nothing of what she had to say.

After a time, when the sun had marched a little longer and the tide had run a little further, the moaning stopped. In the scarred silence, her pitiful face stared far out to where gulls rode the water like swans, and the swans became a legend of bathing maidens whose limbs flashed pale and free in the sunlight. And then she saw that there was a princess with them, a maiden who was bigger and whom the others encircled with love, like a garland. She could taste that love, in the soft salt air of her cell. Then the images were blurred with tears and all she had left was the taste of salt. She folded her arms on her knees, rested her head on her arms and wept, achingly. Life was slipping away with her tears.

Stray thoughts broke through her misery. She realised she might be able to rewrite 'killed' correctly but then worried that it would remain illegible. She thought of leaving a fresh message on a different wall. It would necessarily be a shorter one because there was less space on the walls with the door or the window. When her mind

167

was almost made up and she was ready to write on the stretch of wall to the right of the window, only her name and his and the crucial linking word, she realised what a waste of time it all was. She did not know his name.

He was a deceiver and a liar, a teller of tall tales. He was a man who paid in cash and left no traces. It was inconceivable that he had entrusted her with his true name.

She went over to the stained wall and looked hard at the name she had written. Tom Hoby, a name for a solid English farmer, a name that did not fit him. She tried by the power of concentration to divine the real name behind the disguise. Then her eye ran over the other names. Helen and Carol, Jenny and Kathy, Rusty and Anita. She stroked her fingers over the names, trying to summon to her mind the faces of the women but the images had become a mad jumble.

Defeated, she took up her place at the window. The princess was still swimming, bigger than before which probably made her a queen. Her maidens were chasing along behind her, it was comical how they could not keep up. Linda folded her arms over her knees again, rested her chin on her arms and closed her eyes. Her jacket smelled of blood and decay but she was too cold to take it off and lose the smelly animal heat that it trapped.

She did not look out again until the sun had tramped off to the west and the tide had tickled its way up the beach. The evening was calm, the sea the colour of gunmetal. Mist was enfolding the highest peaks and someone switched on a lamp in a cottage window. Gulls sat like spectres on the rocks. A farmer's daughter was bending over the dead sheep, and a black dog was skittering over the sand towards the barred window, its tail wagging.